Tales Of Old Texas

JW JONES & JOANN MILLER

Hamblen House Publishing

ISBN   979-8-9934642-1-3 Library on Congress Control Number 2025923044

Published by Hamblen House Publishing

Cover design by GetCovers.com

Foreword

This work is directed at those that enjoy history as a story, not just endless dates and vocabulary, but something that lived.

Today, different than the narrator in this tale, we are becoming more and more a cyber connected society. If you read The Tales of Old Texas, kindly give an honest review to Amazon.

Preface

When I was goin' to school over at Midwestern, we had this old history professor named Monihan. Fella could make Texas history walk right into the room and shake your hand. He didn't stand up there and lecture like most people do. He just talked, told stories, one rollin' into the next. You'd be listenin', and before you knew it, class was over. End of class announced, and nobody moved. We all wanted to hear how the story ended.

Now, I don't claim that what follows can take his place, but maybe it'll stir a little of that same feelin'.

Here you'll find an old granddad sittin' on his porch, coffee close at hand and his pipe never far away, tellin' his grandson stories of old Texas. Some of 'em are true; some might've been stretched a bit in the tellin'. But that's porch talk, and that's Texas. Truth and legend sittin' side by side, waitin' on the next sunrise.

And I reckon I'll let the old man keep that last word. He never had much schoolin', but he's got a fine way of speakin' for both of us.

Contents

Prologue

"Where the Wind Still Talks"

He sat on a porch that faced the western sky, where the light fell low and turned everything the color of old pennies. The boards beneath his chair sagged with age, and his overalls had seen better days, faded near white and patched at the knees, carrying the memory of long work done and longer days gone.

His face showed its miles. Deep lines ran from his eyes to the corners of his mouth, and the skin had the look of someone who had spent most of his life outdoors. He wasn't freshly shaved, a trace of gray whiskers roughened his chin, and his expression held the calm of a man who had seen plenty and hurried for nothing.

What hair he had left showed gray in the porch light and stuck out from under a sweat-stained hat that had seen better days. The brim had softened and turned down from years of sun and heat.

Near his boot sat an old enamel mug with chips around the edge and the shine worn off. A thin wisp of steam rose from it, carrying the smell of strong coffee that mixed with the dust and the cool air settling in for the night.

When he spoke, his voice was low and even, touched with the slow drawl of Texas that made a man lean in to catch every word.

"Boy," he said, still watching the horizon, "folks think Texas was built in a day, one flag raised, one speech hollered, and a country born. Ain't so. Took near a century of dust and bad luck, and folks too stubborn to lie down when the Lord said rest."

He leaned forward in his chair, the boards creaking beneath him, and tapped the mug lightly against his knee.

"You see, Texas isn't only a place. "People keep telling the story, and it changes slightly with every telling. The land holds on to what happened here. The hills have seen plenty, and the rivers don't forget. If you sit still, you can hear a bit of it in the wind and in the old leather when it moves."

Now, some of what I'll tell you is written down true, and some of it is memory, passed mouth to mouth until it turned a little smoother around the edges. But a good story doesn't need fixing, it just needs telling."

He tilted back, eyes narrowing as the last of the light slipped away.

"These are the tales of old Texas, the dreamers, the rangers, the cattlemen, the women who stayed, and the fools who thought they could tame it. All gone now, but not forgotten.

So pour a cup, sit yourself down. We'll start at the beginning, with a quiet man named Austin, a stretch of wild land, and three hundred families who thought they'd found paradise."

He smiled then, the wrinkles folding like paper maps.

"Lord help them," he said softly. "They had no idea what they were starting.".

CHAPTER ONE

Austin and His Dream, The Original 300

A Quiet Start

The old man turned the cup in his hands, starin' out where the sun was sinkin'.

"Funny thing," he said. "Every big story, it don't start with gunfire or speeches. It starts quiet. That's how it was with **Stephen F. Austin**. He wasn't the kind they put on horseback in the history books. More of a thinkin' man. Wrote things down, measured before speakin'. Carried his daddy's dream the way a mule hauls a sack, slow, steady, and 'cause somebody had to."

He gave a small chuckle and shook his head. "Now his daddy, **Moses Austin**, he'd already burned through a few lives. Dug lead out of Missouri till the mine gave up on him, tried runnin' a bank that folded faster than a gambler with no cards. Debt chased him clean outta that country.

When most folks would've quit, he got it in his head to try south. Said the land down there was still open, still full of chances."

The chair creaked as he leaned back. "It was 1820. He was old, broke, tired, and too proud to say so. Gray around the temples, boots worn to the stitching. But he saddled up anyway, headin' for Spanish Texas. Said maybe the sun shined different down there. Maybe it'd shine on him." But sometimes the land gives a man one more try."

The boy looked up from his notes. "So he came to Texas?"

The old man nodded. "Rode into Spanish Texas in winter, cold rain followin' him the whole way. Back then, this was still **New Spain**, a quiet country, full of mesquite and missions, and people who didn't take kindly to strangers. He made it to **San Antonio**, lookin' for a governor named **Antonio Martínez**. The guards at the presidio took one look at his worn coat and sent him packin'. To them, he looked like every other desperate drifter who came talkin' about fortunes that didn't exist."

He gave a small grin. "Luck or providence, depends on who you ask, brought him help. A Dutchman named **Baron de Bastrop** had settled here years before. Spoke Spanish, knew everybody who mattered. Bastrop stood up for the old man, told the governor he ought to listen. And Martínez did."

The old man set the cup down, his voice low. "Inside those stone walls, Moses Austin made his pitch. Wanted to bring **three hundred families** from the States, good farmers who'd work the land between the **Brazos** and **Colorado** Rivers. Promised they'd be loyal to Spain, pay their dues, and guard the frontier. Took a lot of talkin', but the governor signed the grant. Right there, the old man got himself a second chance."

He rubbed the arm of his chair, slow and thoughtful. "But the thing about dreams, they don't always wait for the man who dreamed 'em. The ride back north was rough. Rain turned to sleet, sleet to snow. Somewhere on that trail home, Moses caught pneumonia. By the time he reached Missouri, he could barely hold the reins."

The boy's pencil paused. "Did he make it?"

The old man shook his head. "Not quite. He handed the papers to his boy, **Stephen**, and told him, 'Finish what I started.' Then he died. Just like that. Never saw a single acre of the land he'd begged for."

The lantern hissed beside them, throwin' light across the porch rail. "So Stephen buried his father and looked down at that contract. He hadn't planned on leavin' Missouri. Had a mind for law, not for wild country. But a promise is a heavy thing, boy. He packed up the papers and headed south, not for glory, just to keep his word."

The old man drew on his pipe, the coal flarin' in the dark. "That's how Texas started, not with a battle, not with a shout. With a son ridin' into the unknown, chasin' the echo of his daddy's dream."

The Father's Dream

The old man scooted his chair till the back legs thumped solid on the boards. "Now that boy, **Stephen F. Austin**," he said, "he wasn't out to be some hero. Didn't have that in him. He was a book man, raised for papers and talkin' proper, the kind that figures things before speakin'. But when your daddy dies leavin' a promise hangin' in the air, well, you don't get to think it over. You just pack your gear and ride. That's what he did. No fanfare, no music, just a man keepin' his word."

He paused, thumb runnin' along the handle of his mug. "So he packed them papers and rode south. Road was rough, mud and water, more miles than sense. He didn't travel with a parade or a guard, just a horse, a hired hand, and that bundle of dreams folded in a saddlebag. All he had from his pa was a few words and a seal that said *Spain approved.* That, and the kind of determination that don't know when to quit."

He looked toward the boy. "But life's funny about timing. By the time Stephen crossed the border, **Spain** was out, and **Mexico** had taken her place. The flags had changed, uniforms too. He showed up with papers signed by a government that didn't even exist anymore."

The boy blinked. "So what'd he do?"

"What any patient man does," the old man said. "He waited. Met with that Dutch fella again—**Baron de Bastrop**—the same one who'd helped his pa. Bastrop spoke with the new officials, telling them this young man was good for it. Austin kept his hat in his hands and his temper in his pocket till things settled. Weren't many men who could manage that. Most folks would've packed up and gone home."

He tapped the rail with a finger. "Took months, but he got that grant rewritten under the new flag and promised the same thing, **three hundred families**, good farmers, loyal to Mexico now instead of Spain. The land was the same, but the promises had to be new. Austin had a knack for walkin' that fine line between what folks wanted to hear and what was true."

He smiled faintly. "Then he went to see the place himself. Rode down the **Brazos** and **Colorado** rivers, lookin' for what his father had dreamed of. Saw grass waist-high, oak trees thick as a wall, and rivers steady enough to make a man believe. He knew right then the old man hadn't been crazy after all."

The boy wrote something in his notebook. "That's where he started the colony?"

"Right there," the old man said. "Sent word north for settlers, families, not drifters. They came in wagons and flatboats, slow at first, then steady. Hard folks, used to bad luck and worse land. When they crossed the Sabine, they thought they'd found heaven. There was water, soil, and game everywhere. But heaven's a hard landlord."

He leaned back again, the wood poppin' under him. "Austin did what few men could. He brought order to a wilderness. Marked out plots by candlelight, wrote down every name, every boundary. He said a colony could only survive if it had rules, and by God, he kept his own. Made sure every family had a league of land, told 'em to follow Mexican law, stay peaceful with the tribes, and mind their manners. Sounded simple. Never is."

He looked off into the dark yard. "By the time the first cabins went up along the **Brazos**, the sound of axes and hammers carried for miles. That's when Austin wrote home that he believed his father's dream was alive. For a while, it was. You could stand on a ridge and hear the echo of the future."

The boy smiled. "So he made it happen."

The old man nodded slowly. "He did, but he didn't know the price yet. Every dream costs somethin'. Some men just don't find out till it's too late."

The Making of the Colony

The old man poured what was left of the coffee into his cup. "After Austin got the papers settled, folks started comin'," he said. "Not all at once, just a wagon here, a flatboat there. Mostly families from **Tennessee**, **Kentucky**, and **Missouri**. They weren't rich. Just tired of worn-out fields and taxes that never quit."

He rubbed the side of his jaw. "They hauled seed corn, plows, rifles, a couple quilts, maybe a Bible if it didn't weigh too much. Some even dragged milk cows along behind the wagons. They weren't chasin' adventure; they were huntin' a place that might give back what they put in."

The chair groaned as he leaned forward. "Austin met near every one of 'em. Wrote down their names, measured the land by chains and paces, drew maps by candlelight. Said a place without rules turns wild fast. Promised a league and a labor to each family, enough dirt to grow somethin' and still have sky left over. Told 'em to follow **Mexican law**, treat the natives decent if they could, and keep their word. I knowed I said that piece before...it was simple talk, but it worked."

He let out a slow breath. First homes were just one-room log pens, mud between the cracks, a roof that leaked when it rained sideways. No stores. No doctors. When fever hit, it took who it wanted. But they stayed. Cut timber, broke ground, raised corn, and thanked the Lord when it sprouted."

He looked toward the boy. "That's the part people forget, they stayed. Out here, the land'll break you if you don't respect it. Austin told 'em that, and they listened."

He smiled faintly. "He set up a little town on the **Brazos, San Felipe de Austin**: just cabins, a store, a meetin' house. Nothin' fancy, but it was proof the place could hold together. The settlers started callin' him *Empresario.* Spanish for the man in charge. He became the bridge between two tongues, two laws, and two kinds of stubborn."

The pipe clicked against his boot heel. "They called that first crowd the **Old Three Hundred**. Names still show up on markers, **McNeel**, **Kuykendall**, **Bryan**, **Kerr**, **Martin**, **Cummins**. Hard folks, and honest. Didn't know they were plantin' the roots of a state; they just wanted a fair shake."

He gave a nod toward the dark. "They weren't alone, either. Tejano families, **Navarro**, **Seguin**, **de León**, **Enriguez**, **Veramendi**, they were already here. Traded cattle, helped the new folks learn the rivers and the seasons. Without 'em, Austin's dream would've burned out before spring."

The boy asked, "Was it peaceful?"

The old man laughed once. "Peaceful enough to last till sundown. Raids came and went, **Comanche** mostly. Sometimes a stolen horse, sometimes worse. Men kept rifles by the door and dogs under the porch. It wasn't hatred, just survival. Everybody protectin' what was theirs."

He stared into the lantern flame. "Austin rode through it all. From **San Antonio** to the **Colorado**, carryin' letters, settlin' quarrels, remindin' folks they were guests on Mexican soil. He didn't bark orders; he just showed up calm and fair. Folks trusted him for that. Even the soldiers down south gave him his space."

He paused a moment, eyes far away. "He believed in law and patience, two things rare as rain out here. Thought if he could keep both alive, the colony would stand. And for a time, it did. You could walk along the river and hear hammers ringin', smell wood smoke, see cabins glowin' under the trees. For that spell, Texas was young and hopeful."

He knocked his pipe clean. "Didn't stay that way, of course. Never does. But for a few years, it felt like the land itself wanted to help."

The Cost of the Dream

The old man sat quietly for a long while before he spoke again. The only sound was the chair rockin' slow and the wind movin' through the trees.

"Every dream's got a price," he said at last. "Austin's was no different. He gave folks land and law, but the cost came due sooner than anyone wanted to admit."

He rubbed the bowl of his pipe with his thumb. "When them wagons crossed the river, they didn't just bring families. They brought the South with 'em. More than five hundred enslaved folks came with that first bunch. Worked the ground, built cabins, and cleared timber. They did the hardest jobs, and most never saw a sunrise that belonged to them."

The boy looked up. "Didn't Mexico outlaw slavery?"

"Yeah," the old man said. "Had for years. "Mexico had laws, sure," he said, "but laws don't always reach this far out. Austin knew what the paper said. He also knew his folks would pack up if he pushed too hard. So he talked around it, called it *contract work, indenture,* any name that'd keep the peace. Mexico let it slide for a while, and the colony kept breathin'."

He drew a long breath. "Austin wasn't mean, just practical. Maybe too practical. Tried to hold both sides together and near tore himself in half doin' it." Said the colony couldn't make it without that labor. Maybe he was right, maybe not. But it left a mark that never healed. That's the thing about compromise, you think you're keepin' the peace, but sometimes you're just borrowin' trouble."

He leaned forward, elbows on his knees. "Still, they worked. "You could hear axes sing all day," he said. "Hammers long after dark. The land didn't care who swung the tool, only that it got done. Folks worked till their backs gave out."

He scratched his chin, thinking. "When folks got riled, he'd step in quiet," the old man said. "Didn't raise his voice, just talked till they cooled off. Knew near every settler by name, could mark a boundary by the shape of a tree or the bend of a creek. When soldiers down south got jumpy, he'd ride out and talk 'em steady. Most days it worked. Some days it near wore him out."

He scratched his chin, thinking. "He kept things holdin' for a spell, but the cracks were comin'. More wagons crossed the border every season. English words everywhere, songs from back east, flags that didn't match the one flyin' in San Antonio. The officers in Mexico started askin' questions, and not friendly ones."

He paused, lookin' out toward the dark. "After that, the soldiers stayed. More laws came, tighter every year. The settlers grumbled louder. Austin was ridin' himself thin tryin' to hold it all together."

The boy asked softly, "Why didn't he just give up?"

The old man gave a half smile. "That wasn't in him. He'd made his daddy a promise, remember? Promises weigh more than fear. So he kept goin'. Wrote more letters, begged both sides to listen. But talk don't carry far when powder's cheaper than patience."

He leaned back slowly, the chair givin' a tired creak. "By '33, folks out here had reached their limit," he said. "They picked Austin to ride all the way to **Mexico City** and ask for some fairness, less taxes, fewer soldiers, just a little mercy. It was a long ride and a longer wait once he got there. The country was turnin' upside down again, new bosses every few weeks, and each one meaner or more confused than the last." He waited nearly a year, sick half the time, until they told him maybe, just maybe, things would ease."

He looked at the boy and shook his head. "That's how patience ends, quietly, in a cell, a man wonderin' how doin' the right thing went so wrong."

He leaned forward again, elbows on his knees. "Austin waited months down there," he said. "Hot, dusty, sick half the time. Wrote letter after letter tryin' to keep the peace. Thought he'd finally got through, so he sent word home sayin' Texas ought to run its own affairs till Mexico got steady again. That letter got him locked up."

The boy frowned. "For that?"

"Yeah," the old man said. "They called it treason. Hauled him off and threw him in a cell smaller than a corn crib. Stone walls, damp air, little light. He could hear church bells outside and said they sounded like home."

He rubbed his hands together, slowly. "He sat there near a year. When they finally turned him loose, he was thin and gray, but his mind was clear. Rode north through the dry hills, thinkin' the whole way about what was left to save. By the time he reached **San Felipe**, the folks were already talkin' war."

The old man looked at the boy. "They cheered him when he got back, called him a hero. He didn't feel like one. Just looked tired. He told 'em, 'We've tried patience. Now we better be ready for what's next.' "

The chair gave a little groan when he leaned back. "After that, there was no stoppin' it. Muskets fired at **Gonzales**, and the sound rolled clear across the prairie. Austin took command of the army for a bit. Didn't want it, but he did what had to be done. That's who he was."

He drew a long breath. "When the **Convention of '36** met at **Washington-on-the-Brazos**, he was there. Looked older than his years, but he still showed up. After they won independence, they made him Secretary of State. He barely had time to start before the fever took him. Forty-three years old. The Father of Texas gone before his work was half finished."

The old man's eyes followed the wind movin' through the trees. "Sam Houston told the Congress, 'The Father of Texas is no more.' Bells rang all over the settlements that day. Men stood bare-headed in the streets. The land he'd dreamed about was finally free, but he never saw it grow."

He paused, lettin' the night settle. "He never fired the shot that made Texas, but he lit the spark that got it started. Built with patience when others reached for powder. Maybe that's why his name stuck."

He finished his coffee, set the cup down gently, and nodded toward the dark. "Next time," he said, "we'll talk about the ones who were here first, the folks who didn't need a charter or a grant to call this place home. Brave people, proud of their ground."

The lantern hissed, and the porch went quiet again.

CHAPTER TWO

The Land Between Rivers

The night was quiet except for the slow creak of the old man's rocker and the steady chirp of crickets in the trees. The air smelled of mesquite smoke and river mud, and somewhere off in the dark a whip-poor-will called once and fell silent.

The old man leaned forward, elbows on his knees, his pipe glowing faintly in the half-light.

"They say the Brazos was the mother of Texas and the Colorado the father," he began. "Everything between 'em was wild and wide open. Before there were fences, before anybody thought about liberty or flags, this land already had folks who called it home."

He looked at the boy beside him and gave a slow tap on the pipe's bowl.

"People like to say Texas started when Austin brought in his settlers. "That ain't right," he said. "This land already had its own kind of order. The rivers drew the borders, the seasons kept the time, and the stars told a man where he stood."

He took a breath and watched the smoke twist into the dark before speaking again. "My granddaddy used to tell it that way." Said if you stood on a rise between the Brazos and the Colorado, you could feel the whole country breathing, the forests in the east, the grasslands to the west, the salt air off the Gulf. Said the rivers were old before any mapmaker ever dipped a pen in ink. Folks forget that."

He looked off across the pasture, where the moonlight caught the tops of the mesquites.

He took a slow breath before he spoke again. "This land wasn't empty," he said. "It just carried other names back then. In the east, you had the **Caddo**, farmin' the pine woods. Down on the coast were the **Karankawa**, fishin' and huntin' along the bays. Out on the flat country, the **Comanche** rode the wind, fast and quiet. The **Wichita**, **Kiowa**, and **Apache** shared that same stretch of sky when they could. And later the **Cherokee** came down from the hills, worn out and hopin' for just a little peace. All of 'em fit in this place better than we ever have."

The boy shifted on the step. "You ever seen any of their old camps?"

The old man nodded slowly. "A few. You can find traces if you know where to look, a scatter of flint chips near a creek, a circle of stones where a fire once burned. The rivers keep their secrets, but they don't keep 'em well. Every spring flood turns up somethin' older than the towns built on top of it."

He reached for the coffeepot, poured a small measure into his cup, and took a sip.

"This land between the rivers, that's where Texas started, long before the word existed. The settlers didn't make Texas; they just gave new names to old places. What came later, the fights, the ranches, the flags, all of it grew out of this ground."

He leaned back in his chair, the wood creaking beneath him.

"Listen closely, now. I'll tell you about the world before the wagons rolled, when the rivers were the only roads a man could follow. That's where the story begins."

The Old World

The old man tapped the bowl of his pipe against the rail, the sound sharp in the stillness.

"Before there were settlers or flags or talk of freedom," he said, "this land already had a life of its own. The rivers fed it, the wind taught it, and the people listened."

He looked out across the pasture as if he could still see it the way it was.

"Up east, the **Caddo** worked the rich bottomland. They built towns out of poles and clay, planted corn and beans, and stored grain in tall huts that could keep a man fed through winter. They traded salt, pottery, and hides from one river to the next. They called this country

Taysha, which means 'friend'. The Spaniards turned it into Texas. Funny thing how a word for friendship ended up naming so many battles."

He took a draw from his pipe and nodded toward the south.

"Down along the coast lived the **Karankawa**. Tall people, broad in the shoulders, used to the salt and sun. They fished the bays, hunted deer, and paddled canoes through the marshes. When storms rolled in off the Gulf, they moved inland to the oak woods and waited it out. Folks later called them wanderers, but they weren't wanderin', they were followin' the tides and the seasons, same as the wind."

The boy leaned forward a little. "Were they dangerous?"

The old man gave a slow shrug.

"When they had to be. Any people will fight if you corner 'em. They didn't go lookin' for trouble, but they knew what to do when it found 'em."

He pointed west, the pipe stem tracing a line toward the dark horizon.

"Out past the trees stretched **Comanchería**, the country of the **Comanche**. That was a world all its own. They rode lean ponies and moved faster than the wind itself. Could fire a bow from a gallop, hangin' off the side of a horse, and hit what they aimed at. They ruled those plains because nobody else could. Their herds ran farther than a man could count. They traded when it suited them, fought when it didn't, and every traveler who crossed that prairie learned one thing, the Comanche made the rules out there."

He sat quietly for a long moment, watching the smoke drift and fade.

"Between those big nations were others. The **Tonkawa** kept to the rivers, huntin' deer and buffalo and sometimes guidin' strangers who paid 'em fair. The **Lipan Apache** fought most everyone, movin' west when they had to. The **Wichita** farmed and traded up north, and the **Kiowa** shared the plains with the Comanche, friends one season and enemies the next. Each people had their way, their ground, their own truth."

He turned his gaze east again.

"And then came the **Cherokee**. They were the last to arrive. Got pushed out of their own country back in the States, thought they'd find peace here. Built farms near Nacogdoches, planted peaches and corn, raised cabins like the ones they'd left behind. For a while, it worked."

The boy said nothing, only listened to the steady creak of the rocker.

The old man spoke more softly now.

"My granddaddy told me the world was quieter then. The nights were darker, the stars brighter, and a man could hear his own thoughts in the wind. Those people lived by that wind. They took what they needed, thanked the land,

and left the rest alone. You can't say that for the ones who came later."

He leaned back and looked toward the distant line of trees.

"That was Texas before the wagons, a country full of life, not emptiness. Folks today still call it wilderness, but that means they never learned the names of the people who were already here."

He knocked the ash from his pipe and poured another cup of coffee.

"Now, boy," he said, "that's the old world. Next came the meetin', two kinds of folks tryin' to share one stretch of ground. It started with handshakes and ended with gun smoke. That's where we'll pick it up.

The Meeting of Worlds

The old man rubbed a thumb along the stem of his pipe before he spoke again.

"When the settlers came," he said, "they didn't come swingin' rifles. Most of 'em came with plows and prayers. They were lookin' for good dirt and clean water, not war. But they stepped into a world that already had its own ways, and they didn't know enough to listen."

He leaned back, the chair creaking.

"The Brazos and the Colorado were the first trails that tied the old life to the new. Settlers built cabins on their banks, right where the tribes had camped for generations. You'd find **Caddo** traders there, carryin' corn and pottery, swappin' for iron pots, cloth, and powder. The **Tonkawa** showed newcomers which roots were safe to eat, where to dig for fresh water, and what the weather meant when the birds flew low. Even the **Comanche**, proud as they were, came to trade horses and hides for tobacco and sugar. The first markets weren't in towns; they were under trees along the riverbanks."

He paused long enough to fill his pipe and light it again.

"For a while, it worked fine. There was respect in the air then, maybe not trust, but enough patience to share a meal and a fire. The winters were cruel, and survival didn't care much for skin color or language. A hungry man's just a hungry man."

The story widened out in his voice.

"As more families came in, things started changin'. They cut timber for fences and cleared fields for corn. To them, it was life. To the tribes, it was takin' away somethin' sacred. Buffalo herds began movin' west, and with 'em went the deer and antelope. The hunters found themselves ridin' farther every season, and the settlers filled the ground they left behind."

The boy stirred on the porch step. "Didn't they see what they were doin'?"

The old man gave a slow shake of his head.

"Maybe they did, but they figured it couldn't be helped. Folks from the States were used to laws and boundaries on paper. Out here, the land didn't pay much mind to paper. It belonged to whoever could hold it that day."

He turned toward the dark pasture, eyes far away.

"Trouble started small. A few horses missin', maybe a couple of steers gone. Then came a burned cabin, a raid at dawn, a settler's body found on the trail. Nobody knew who struck first, and after that it didn't matter. The young men on both sides were eager to prove somethin', and pride's a dangerous fuel."

He drew on his pipe, the glow catching the lines of his face.

"In **San Felipe**, Stephen F. Austin tried to stop it before it got out of hand. He sent riders to the tribal camps, asked for peace, and offered a trade fair. He told the settlers to hold their fire and remember that fear makes fools of decent men. But fear travels faster than a letter can, and by the time his words reached the frontier, the smoke from a dozen burned cabins was already risin' into the sky."

He set the pipe aside.

"There was one winter when it near held together," the old man said. "The **Tonkawa** helped wagon trains cross the flooded creeks. The **Caddo** showed up with corn when the crops went bad. Even a few **Comanche** came to trade. For a little while, folks shared the land and quit shootin' long enough to breathe." Then spring came, and new wagons rolled in, cuttin' fresh trails and plantin' fences where the hunters used to camp. The circle started again."

The boy's voice was small. "Did they ever talk things through?"

"They tried," the old man said. "Austin met with chiefs, smoked pipes, promised friendship. The chiefs nodded polite like, but both sides knew talk only goes so far when the ground itself is the prize. You can't roam and farm the same land at the same time. One way or another, someone's got to move."

He took a swallow of coffee, then leaned forward, elbows on his knees.

"There were nights the settlers slept in groups, keepin' watch with rifles on their laps. You'd hear the dogs bark out toward the river and everybody'd freeze, listenin'. Sometimes it was nothin'. Sometimes it was the last sound a man ever heard. They called it the price of progress, though progress always seems to charge the same coin."

He rubbed his jaw, slow and thoughtful.

"Not all of it was hate. Some learned from each other. A few **Tonkawa** boys went to school in the settlements. A couple of young settlers joined the hunts, speakin' broken bits of Comanche and bringin' meat back for the winter. There were friendships made out there, small ones, quiet ones, but they never lasted long enough to outlive the fear."

He looked over at the boy.

"That's how it goes, son. Two worlds meet, and the strong one don't always win, just the one that can stand still the longest. The settlers had walls and plows; the tribes had horses and memory. The land could've held 'em both if pride hadn't gotten in the way."

The wind picked up, rustling through the pecans behind the house.

"Most folks think the story of Texas starts with the Revolution," he said softly. "It really started here, on the banks of the Brazos, in the dark before dawn, when men decided they couldn't share the same ground anymore. That's when the peace died, quiet as an ember in the wind."

He leaned back, pipe resting cold in his hand.

"Remember that, boy," he said. "History ain't built on victory. It's built on what people lose tryin' to keep what's theirs."

The Coming of the Storm

The old man drew a long breath and stared toward the horizon, where a thin fog had settled over the pasture.

"Peace don't last long on a border," he said. "By the mid-thirties, the calm was gone. Wagons kept comin', fences went up, and the talk got louder. The land filled up with new names and new rules, and it started to push back."

He rubbed the bowl of his pipe with his thumb.

"Up in the east, the **Cherokee** were tryin' to hold on to the small bit they had left. They'd built good farms near Nacogdoches, planted corn and peaches, even had mills turnin' on the creeks. Their chief, **Duwali**, folks called him Chief Bowl, trusted **Sam Houston**, who'd once lived among 'em and swore they'd be treated fair. They called him the Raven. But promises written on paper don't last long when land starts runnin' short."

He leaned forward, the chair creaking under him.

"Then there was the **Fredonian business**. Haden Edwards and his men down around Nacogdoches got it in their heads to pull loose from Mexico before anyone else was ready. Called it the Republic of Fredonia, but it didn't last long. The **Cherokee** got blamed for helpin', though most stayed clear of it. Austin had to ride east and settle it down himself. That was the first crack in the wall."

The boy frowned. "Was it really a war?"

"Not yet," the old man said. "But it showed what was comin'. Mexico started sendin' more soldiers north, and the settlers started talkin' rebellion. Folks forgot about the neighbors they'd traded with and started seein' enemies behind every tree line. Fear's quicker than any messenger."

He took a drink of coffee and looked out into the dark.

"Some of the tribes packed up and moved north toward the Red River. Others stayed, hopin' the storm would pass. The **Comanche** didn't move at all. They'd seen empires rise and fall before. They figured this one would, too."

He tapped the side of his pipe, lost in thought.

"When the war with Mexico finally came in thirty-five, most of the tribes stayed out of it. They'd already buried too many of their own fightin' other people's battles. But when the smoke cleared and Texas called itself a republic, the new government began drawin' lines on maps like the land was empty. Surveyors drove stakes into old hunting grounds. Deeds were printed faster than fences could be built. Paper changed hands quicker than horses."

He paused and shook his head.

"Houston tried to hold the peace when he was president. He met with the chiefs, offered trade, and begged the settlers to keep their guns shouldered. But a man's word don't reach far when the country's bigger than his voice. Out west, the **Comanche** raids kept comin'. Down east, the **Cherokee** got pushed off the farms they'd built. In thirty-nine, the Republic sent soldiers to drive them north. The fight at the **Neches River** ended it. Chief Bowl was killed, and the rest crossed into Indian Territory. That was the last of the Cherokee in Texas."

The old man's voice softened, and the wind filled the silence for a moment.

"The **Karankawa** were gone by then, scattered or dead. The **Caddo** had been pushed into Louisiana. Only the **Comanche** and **Kiowa** still rode free, and even they knew it couldn't last. Roads cut across old trails, and towns rose where camps once stood. You could hear church bells where the coyotes used to call."

He looked at the boy, eyes steady in the dim light.

"Every country's born out of someone's dream and someone else's sorrow. That's the truth of Texas. The land between the Brazos and the Colorado gave birth to both, the dream that built it and the sorrow it was built over."

He nodded toward the dark.

The old man fell quiet. The pipe had gone cold in his hand, and the night was still enough to hear the frogs down by the creek. A soft wind came off the pasture, stirring the lantern flame and carrying the smell of damp earth and cedar.

After a long minute, he said, "That's how it was, boy. The land rememberin' every step, every name, every promise that ever got broke. People came and went, but the rivers stayed. They've seen it all and don't tell much about it. You can hear a bit if you listen right, though, in the sound of water over rock or in the wind when it turns before a storm."

He leaned back in his chair, the boards creakin' beneath him.

"Texas didn't start with flags or speeches. It started with people learnin' and forgettin' how to live with this ground. All that came later, the fights, the heroes, the songs, they were just echoes of this place tryin' to teach us who we are."

The boy nodded, eyes wide in the dim light.

The old man smiled faintly, a corner of his mouth twitching under the shadow of his hat.

"Tomorrow," he said, "we'll talk about the ones who carried that dream forward. The fighters. The loud ones. The men who believed freedom was worth dyin' for."

He reached for the coffeepot, poured the last of it into his cup, and watched the steam rise.

"Best get some sleep," he said softly. "Mornin's comin', and the next part of the story don't wait on anyone."

The boy nodded again, and the porch fell still except for the faint creak of the chair and the low hum of the night beyond the rails.

CHAPTER THREE

"You Can Go to Hell, I'm Going to Texas"

The old man eased back in his chair and watched a moth chase the lantern light.

"Davy Crockett wasn't made for quiet rooms," he said. "He was at his best in places where the ground was rough and the sky was wide. Folks knew him from stories long before they knew him as a man. One story said that he killed a bear by grinnin' it to death. Some of those stories were true. Some were just big enough to fit his name."

He tipped the pipe and let a curl of smoke drift into the dark.

"When Tennessee turned its back on him and didn't reelect him to Congress, he didn't argue much. He just stood up in a tavern, told the crowd they could do as they pleased, and said he was goin' to Texas. He meant it. A man gets one or two fresh starts in a life, and he aimed to take his."

He looked at the boy.

"People think he came huntin' glory. He didn't. He was huntin' a place where a man's word still counted. Texas had a way of promisin' that. It also had a way of collectin' more than it gave."

He set the pipe down and folded his hands.

"Listen close. I'll tell you how he rode west, how he walked through the gates of the old mission, and how the story everyone remembers started with a fiddle, a cold wind, and a short supply of powder."

The Road to Texas

Crockett left Tennessee in late 1835 with three companions and not much else. William Patton, Abner Burgin, and Lyman Curtis rode with him. The weather was bad, the rivers were higher than usual, and the miles stretched like rope. He kept a small journal and wrote in a plain hand. The entries were short. A night under a shed roof. A meal someone would not pay for. Rain. More rain.

They crossed into Arkansas as winter settled in. The trail was slick, and the air cut like a knife. Some nights they slept dry. Most nights, they didn't. He talked easily with strangers, traded stories for food, and picked at a fiddle when someone put one in his hands. People liked him because he listened first and laughed last.

By January, they reached Nacogdoches. The town leaned against the pines and carried two languages in the same breath. Crockett walked into a room where papers were laid out on a table, and a few men in rough coats waited. He signed his name to a pledge to serve Texas for six months. He did not ask what it would cost. No one in that room knew enough to tell him.

The Old Man's voice slid back in for a moment.

"Some men talk about destiny," he said. "Crockett talked about miles. He knew the only way out was forward."

From Nacogdoches, they turned west. The land opened, and the trees thinned. They followed the old road that ran toward San Antonio. Coyotes paced the edges of their campfires. The air went hard at night, and the grass snapped under the horses' hooves at dawn. They shot what they could, bought what they could not shoot, and carried little more than rifles, blankets, and a pair of kettles.

They reached the Guadalupe and crossed in cold water up to the saddle skirts. Other men fell in with them along the way. Some had heard the call for volunteers, some were just hungry for a new place to stand. Talk drifted through the camps that a large Mexican army had crossed the Rio Grande and was marching north under Santa Anna. Crockett listened, then tuned the fiddle and played a tune he knew from back home. A few men sang. Most just stared into the fire.

They rode into San Antonio in early February. The town looked tired and half empty. Stone walls and sun-baked adobes threw back a thin winter light. The old mission they called the Alamo stood at its edge, a rough fort patched with dirt and timber. The walls were long, much too long for the few men inside to defend. Men were already at work to try and make it more . They dragged timbers, shoveled earth, and stacked powder where it would keep dry. They had a few small cannons.

Crockett set his bedroll near a wall and shook hands with the officers. William Barret Travis was young and sharp as a new knife. James Bowie looked older than his years and carried a sickness that would not leave him. "No man is all good or evil, and Bowie surely fit that bill. Stories says he made a tidy sum smugglin' slaves into Louisianna, helped by the pirate, Lafitte. Who knows, but when the chips were in the pot, Bowie stayed. Maybe, after the death of his family to illness, he was ready, only him and the wind know for sure. They both welcomed Crockett because a famous name could help hold a thin line, and because the man behind the name looked like someone who would not run.

The Old Man's voice came back, soft.

"He didn't make speeches," he said. "He set to work. That's the kind of talk the frontier understands."

Days slid into the same shape. They patched the palisade. They molded bullets from scavenged lead. Crockett and a few others slipped out to hunt when it was safe and brought back thin deer or a brace of birds. At night, he drew a bow across the strings, played a slow air, then something that made men smile for a minute. He slept in his coat with his rifle within reach.

On the twenty-third of February, dust rose to the south. Scouts came in fast with the word. Lines of green coats, white cross belts bright in the cold light, and drums under the noise of feet. Santa Anna's army had arrived. The Texans fell back into the mission and barred the gates. A white flag did not rise over the walls that day.

The first rounds from the Mexican cannon shook dirt from the old stones. The defenders answered with what they had. Then the long wait began.

The Old Man paused long enough to pour a little coffee and taste it.

"That's how sieges work," he said. "Noise, then quiet. Fear, then chores. A man keeps busy or he breaks."

Inside the Alamo, men found work where they could. If they were not on the wall, they hauled water, fixed gear, or sat with a boy who had never heard guns that close and talked him steady. Letters were written by candle stub. Travis sent one out that asked for help. He ended it with words that would outlive him. Some messengers got through. Most did not come back.

Each night, the cannon spoke, and the walls shed dust. Each morning, the flags still hung where they had been hung the day before. Crockett kept his corner of the line and did not say much. A man who has to prove he is brave is not. He had nothing left to prove.

Inside the Alamo: Days of Waiting and Resolve

The first nights of the siege were a mix of noise and silence. Cannonballs hit the outer wall, and dust drifted down like powder snow. When the guns paused, the only sound was wind pushing through the gaps in the old stones.

The old man set his cup down and looked at the boy.

"Those men didn't expect to live through it," he said. "But they meant to make the cost too high to forget."

Inside the mission, Travis moved along the line, checking men and guns. He was young and carried himself like it. His coat was worn, his voice steady. Bowie lay in a cot in the long barracks, a knife within reach, fever sweat on his face. He'd promised to fight from the bed if he had to. Crockett stayed near the palisade, quiet as ever, rifle across his knees.

Travis wrote another letter, this one to all of Texas. The candle burned low while he scratched out the words. He asked for reinforcements and ended with a line that would echo through generations: "I shall never surrender or retreat." He signed it "Victory or Death."

The Old Man's voice slipped back through the telling.

"You can talk about pride or bravery, but what Travis wrote was a kind of prayer. He knew no one was comin' in time. He just wanted the world to know they'd chosen how to die."

A few nights later, he gathered the men in the courtyard. The cannon had gone quiet, and the air smelled of powder and sweat. Bowie was carried out on his cot so he could hear him. Travis spoke plainly: Santa Anna's army was tightening the circle, and no help had come. He drew his sword across the dirt and told every man what it meant: cross the line and stay, or walk away while there was still dark enough to hide.

The old man paused, his pipe forgotten in his hand.

"Some say every man stepped over," he said. "Some say one didn't. Doesn't matter. The point is, they all knew the choice. Most stayed. That's what courage looks like when you strip it down, decidin' to stay put when walkin' off would be easier."

Days blurred. The defenders patched holes, shared what food was left, and counted the shells that hadn't split open. At night, Crockett played the fiddle to keep the fear from echoing too loud. A few men tried to sleep. Others just watched the stars and wondered who'd see them next.

Then word came that help was on the way, the **Gonzales Volunteers**, thirty-two men from the town that had once told Mexico Come and Take It when asked to surrender the towns cannon. They'd hauled that same stubbornness all the way to San Antonio. They slipped through enemy lines on a cold night and joined the garrison. No one cheered; there wasn't a breath to waste. But for a little while, the sound of their boots in the courtyard made the place feel less alone.

The old man nodded slowly.

"That's the kind of thing Texas was built on. Folks fightin' with more heart than numbers. The Gonzales boys brought that spirit with 'em, the same one that stood behind that cannon and dared an army to come get it."

Santa Anna's guns fired heavily each day. The Mexican flag of no quarter flew above their lines. Bugles sounded " el DeGuello', emphasizing Santa Anna's order, an order for no quarter to be given to the defenders. Inside, men shared the last of the cornmeal and water. Travis split what powder they had into small sacks and handed them out like communion.

The old man's voice dropped low.

"They were already ghosts by then, but they didn't act like it. They cleaned their rifles, patched their coats, and waited for dawn."

He looked at the boy.

"Remember, son, bravery ain't loud. It's a man checkin' his gun and noddin' to his friend when both know what's comin'."

The Fall and the Fire That Followed

The old man's voice dropped low, the sound of it almost blending with the night wind.

"March the sixth, eighteen thirty-six," he said. "That was the morning it all came due."

Before dawn, a cold mist hung over the mission. Inside the walls, men were still half asleep when the bugles sounded. Santa Anna's army moved in four columns, shadows thick enough to hide behind. The first wave came at the north wall, ladders clattering, muskets flashing in the dark.

Travis was on the rampart, his pistol in one hand and sword in the other. He fired once, shouted for his men to stand fast, and fell where he stood. The cannon on the plaza tore gaps through the attackers, but they kept coming. The air filled with smoke, screams, and the sound of boots on stone.

The boy spoke softly. "Did they ever have a chance?"

The old man shook his head.

"Not really. But that wasn't the point."

In the courtyard, Bowie's cot had been moved near a wall. He was too sick to stand. The women survivors said he fired pistols from the bed until the smoke hid him. No one knows how many he took with him, but every man knew he would never ask for mercy.

The old man's voice was sad as he continued. "Crockett and a few others held the chapel. They fired till the powder ran out and fought with whatever was left in reach, rifles used as clubs, knives, and bare hands. By sunrise, the fight was done. The old walls were lined with bodies, blue-gray coats, and homespun shirts, all mixed together in the dust. Ours, theirs, don't make no never mind to the dead"

The old man stared into the dark yard beyond the porch rail.

"There are stories about how Crockett died," he said. "Some say he fell fightin' at the door. Others say he was taken alive and shot after. Truth is, nobody knows. Doesn't matter. What matters is that he stayed. All of 'em did."

He took a long breath.

"Santa Anna ordered the bodies burned. Smoke from the pyres drifted over the town for two days. Folks said you could smell it ten miles out. And while that smoke rose, the rest of Texas was listenin'."

He tapped the edge of his pipe against his boot heel.

"News of the Alamo spread slow at first, then like fire through dry grass. Men dropped their plows, saddled horses, and rode for Houston's camp. They weren't ridin' for revenge, not just that. They were ridin' to prove that all those who'd died in that mission hadn't done it for nothin'."

He looked over at the boy.

"You see, the Alamo wasn't a loss, not really. It was a voice. It said to every man who heard it: Hold your ground."

The boy was quiet for a long time.

"What about the Mexicans?" he asked. "Didn't they fight for somethin' too?"

The old man nodded slowly.

"They did. They fought for orders, for a flag, for the idea of their own country stayin' whole. War don't give one side a patent on courage. There were brave men on both ends of that field, and most of 'em never asked to be there. That's the hard part to remember."

He reached for the coffeepot, poured the last swallow, and sipped it before going on.

"After the Alamo, Texas changed. The people weren't talkin' about land anymore. They were talkin' about freedom, about standin' on their own feet. You can draw all the maps you want, but a country starts in the hearts of folks who've had enough."

The wind stirred the trees beyond the fence.

"When they rode to San Jacinto a few weeks later, some carried scraps of cloth representing the Alamo in their pockets. Others just carried the memory. That was enough to turn a fight into a cause."

He leaned back in his chair, eyes on the horizon where no light remained.

"Crockett never made it home, but his words did. 'You can go to hell, I'm goin' to Texas.' Folks still say it, though most don't remember the weight behind it. He wasn't cursin' anyone. He was pickin' a side."

The boy looked up at him. "Would you have stayed?"

The old man smiled faintly, lines deepening around his eyes.

"Don't know," he said. "A man never truly knows what he'd do till the hour comes. But I'd like to think I'd have stepped over that line with the rest."

He knocked the ashes from his pipe and watched them scatter on the porch.

"That's the Alamo, son. No speeches, no heroes, just men standin' where they said they would, no matter what came next. The kind of stand that builds legends and costs everything."

He let the chair rock once more, the sound soft against the night.

"Next time, I'll tell you about the tough times the Texians faced, short on everythin' but guts."

CHAPTER FOUR

Before San Jacinto: Fannin, Goliad, and the Runaway Scrape

The fire in the tin lantern had burned low. The old man stirred the coals in his pipe but didn't bother to light it. He just watched the smoke curl away from the bowl, thin as memory.

"After the Alamo," he said, "it felt like Texas had died with it. The fight at that old mission took the best men we had, and the rest of the country didn't know what to do next. News came slow, but when it came, it came heavy."

He leaned forward, elbows on his knees.

"Santa Anna didn't stop at San Antonio. He split his army and sent columns east, burnin' towns and raisin' that red flag meanin' no mercy. The settlers started packin' up before the dust from his boots even settled. Men rode off to join Sam Houston's army, leavin' families to fend for themselves. Women hitched up oxen, loaded wagons, and pointed east, hopin' to stay ahead of the smoke."

The boy frowned. "You mean they ran?"

"They ran," the old man said. "And they were right to. Ain't shame in runnin' when the wind's against you. Houston knew it, too. He told his men the same thing my granddaddy used to say about a flood , 'You don't stop it; you outlast it.' But folks didn't see it that way then. They just saw their homes goin' up in flames."

He reached for his coffee, took a sip, and set the cup back down.

"While the people were runnin', another fight was brewin' farther west. A man named **James Fannin** was sittin' at a place called Goliad with near four hundred men. They were supposed to pull back, but orders came late, and pride came early. He waited too long, and by the time he packed up, the Mexicans had him boxed in."

The old man sighed, the sound deep and rough.

"That's where the story turns dark, boy. The Alamo was brave. Goliad was cruel. Texas needed both to understand what it was fightin' for."

He looked toward the dark beyond the porch, where the river fog was startin' to rise.

"Some stories come with flags and drums. Others come with smoke and silence. This one's the latter."

He leaned back, eyes on the horizon.

"Let's start with Fannin and the men who never made it home. Then we'll talk about the ones who ran, and how that run turned into the last march of the war."

Fannin and the Massacre at Goliad

The old man tamped the tobacco in his pipe, struck a match, and let it burn down before he spoke.

"After the Alamo, Santa Anna kept movin' east," he said. "He wanted to crush every pocket of resistance before the settlers could gather. He sent General **José de Urrea** down the coast, a good soldier by most accounts, quick, disciplined, and merciless when the orders said to be. Urrea's path led him straight to **Goliad**."

He looked off into the dark.

"There at Goliad sat **James Walker Fannin**, a Georgian by birth, a dreamer by temperament. He was holdin' the old Spanish fort, the **Presidio La Bahía**, with about four hundred men, rough volunteers, a few trained soldiers, the rest farmers with rifles. His orders from Sam Houston were simple enough: fall back to **Victoria** and join the main army. But Fannin hesitated. Some say he wanted to bring out the cannon and supplies. Others say he was waitin' on friends who never came. Whatever the reason, the clock ran out on him."

The old man leaned forward, voice low and even.

"On the morning of March nineteenth, Fannin finally broke camp. They loaded the wagons heavy with ammunition and baggage. The oxen were slow, the sun high.

They'd gone no more than ten miles when they hit a stretch of open prairie near **Coleto Creek**. That's where Urrea found 'em."

He tapped the pipe against the rail.

"It was a wide, flat plain with no trees, no cover, and grass barely high enough to hide a rabbit. Urrea's cavalry came ridin' in like a storm. Fannin drew his men and wagons into a square, rifles at the ready, cannon on the flanks. The fight started late in the day and ran till near sundown. The Mexicans charged again and again, but every time they came close, the Texans fired and drove 'em back. The smoke hung thick over the grass, and the ground was slick with blood on both sides. Fannin caught a bullet through the thigh early on but kept shoutin' orders from where he lay. By dark, the wounded outnumbered the well."

The boy's voice was small in the quiet. "Did they hold?"

"They did," the old man said, "for that day. They spent the night listenin' to the moans of the hurt and the clatter of Mexican troops gettin' ready to hit 'em again. "When the sun came up, it was red as blood," the old man said. "Urrea had his cannon ready, and the Texans gave back what little fire they had left. By then, their water was gone, powder near the same. Fannin called his officers over, talked low for a bit, and then sent word to Urrea. The Mexican general promised fair treatment if they gave up. Fannin took him at his word. Some folks say he was fooled, others say he was just out of choices. Either way, the shootin' stopped, and that field went still."

He drew on his pipe, the ember glowing like a coal in the dark.

"They were marched back to Goliad, back to that old presidio. The walls there are thick limestone, sun-bleached and stubborn. You can still see 'em standin' today, the **Presidio La Bahía**. For a week, those men waited inside. Some of the men tended the wounded, some prayed, some scratched notes for families they'd never see again. They thought they'd be exchanged or sent north. Urrea himself argued for mercy, but Santa Anna's orders came down clear: every prisoner to be executed. No exceptions."

He let the words hang, the porch settling into silence except for the sound of night insects in the grass.

"Palm Sunday morning, March twenty-seventh, 1836. The prisoners were roused at dawn, fed a little bread, and divided into three groups. The guards said they were bein' moved. The first column marched down the Victoria road, the second toward the river, the third west across the prairie. When they were far enough from the fort, the soldiers halted. Then the guards stepped back, leveled their muskets, and fired."

He took a slow sip of coffee before going on.

"Some dropped where they stood. Others ran, but the cavalry rode 'em down. A few dove into the brush and lay under the bodies till nightfall. About thirty men escaped, helped by Mexicans who couldn't stand the slaughter. Back at the presidio, the wounded, Fannin among them, were kept in the courtyard. He asked to be shot in the heart, not the head, and to have his watch sent home to his family. They granted him that much. When the volley came, he died sittin' up straight."

The boy swallowed hard. "All that for followin' orders?"

The old man nodded slowly.

"Sometimes orders are just words a man follows till he runs out of luck. Fannin did his duty, and it cost him every man he had."

He leaned back in the chair, eyes half closed.

"After the smoke cleared, the bodies were burned in piles, the ashes driftin' on the wind. The fort stood quiet again, like it was holdin' its breath. When folks talk about Goliad now, they remember the fight at Coleto Creek, four hundred men fightin' with no water and no shade, but the real story's what came after. The massacre broke whatever hope Texas had left. Some called for surrender. Others clenched their fists. Either way, nobody would ever forget it."

He knocked his pipe against the rail, the sound echoing like a shot.

"Houston was right when he said those ashes lit the road to **San Jacinto**. You can't burn men like that and not set the whole country on fire."

He looked toward the horizon as if he could still see the old walls standing against the dawn.

"I've been to that presidio, boy. Stone's still cool even in July. The place feels heavy, like the air won't move. Some folks say they can hear the wind whistle through the archways at night. I've heard it myself. It don't sound like wind to me. Sounds more like names."

The Runaway Scrape

The old man's pipe had gone out again, but he kept it in his hand, turnin' it slow between his fingers.

"After Goliad," he said, "the whole country came apart. Word of the Alamo had been bad enough, but Goliad broke folks clean through. Santa Anna was marchin' east, and every town in his path knew what that meant."

He leaned forward, elbows on his knees.

"People took what they could carry," the old man said. "Some hooked up oxen to wagons. Others threw bundles on saddle horses. A few just started down the road on foot. They left the plows in the rows and the fires still burnin' in the hearth. Chickens ran wild in the yards, and dogs followed a ways before givin' up. Nobody looked back much. They just kept movin', listenin' for hoofbeats behind 'em."

He nodded toward the east, as if he could still see the line of wagons stretching that way.

"They called it the **Runaway Scrape,** whole towns movin' at once, Gonzales, San Felipe, Victoria, Bastrop.

The roads turned to mud from the rains, and every river they came to was swollen. Wagons bogged down, oxen gave out, people waded through water up to their chests carryin' children and whatever food they had left. Some drowned. Some froze in the cold rain. But most just kept movin'."

He took a breath, the sound rough. "My great-grand-mother was a girl then. She told me her family crossed the Brazos on a raft made from doors and fence rails. Said they lost half their things to the current. They stopped on the far bank, built a fire out of wet wood, and called that survival."

The boy asked, "Wasn't there an army to protect them?"

"There was," the old man said. "What was left of it. Sam Houston was pullin' back, gatherin' what men he could. He told 'em they couldn't fight Santa Anna yet, too few guns, too little powder. Most called him a coward for it. They wanted a hero, not a strategist. But Houston was buyin' time, waitin' for the land itself to help him. He knew the rivers and the mud would slow the enemy more than bullets could."

He looked at the boy.

"Sometimes winnin' starts with runnin' the right way."

He leaned back again, pipe forgotten.

"The army and the people moved together for weeks. You could stand on a ridge and see the dust of the wagons stretch to the horizon. Behind that line came fire, towns burnin' so the Mexicans couldn't use what was left. Every few miles, someone would stop, turn a wagon crosswise, and make a stand till Houston's scouts rode through tellin' 'em to move on."

He reached for the coffee pot, poured what was left, and stared into the cup.

"There were small kindnesses along that road. A woman givin' her last bit of cornmeal to a stranger. A preacher baptizin' a baby in a muddy creek. Old men liftin' children onto wagons when their legs gave out. Folks were scared, but they didn't turn mean. That counts for somethin'."

He looked out toward the pasture where the night fog was rolling in.

"By April, they'd crossed the Trinity and reached the east edge of the state. Some talked about leavin' Texas for good, crossin' into Louisiana. Houston stopped at a place called Groce's Landing on the Brazos and started trainin' what he had, a thousand men, give or take. No uniforms, few shoes, but they were Texans through and through. He drilled 'em, waited, and listened. All the while, Santa Anna was splittin' his army to chase ghosts."

The boy leaned forward. "So Houston was runnin' on purpose?"

The old man smiled faintly.

"He was. He was lettin' Santa Anna stretch his line thin as a lariat. Houston knew that once the general got far enough from his supply, the land would turn on him. The rivers, the mud, and the people's anger, that's what he was countin' on."

He tapped the rail with one finger.

"The **Runaway Scrape** looked like defeat, but it wasn't. It was the breath before the shout, the bend in the bow before the arrow flies. Texas was gatherin' itself, even if nobody knew it then."

He took a long look toward the dark east.

"Next time you drive the highway past San Felipe or cross the Brazos near Richmond, remember that road. Under all that asphalt is the path of a people runnin' for their lives and findin' their country at the same time."

Santa Anna Splits His Forces

The old man refilled his cup and let the steam rise before speaking again.

"While the settlers were runnin' for their lives," he said, "two generals were playin' a game of patience and pride. One knew the land. The other thought he owned it."

He leaned forward, pipe still unlit in his hand.

"Sam Houston was marchin' east with what passed for an army , farmers with rifles, merchants with muskets, boys too young to shave. They were mad, tired, and ready to quit him. Every mile they went, they saw more families on the road, and every face asked the same question: 'When are we gonna fight?' Houston just told 'em, 'Not yet.'"

He smiled faintly.

"Now, Santa Anna couldn't stand the word wait. He figured victory was his for the takin'. He was a prideful man, would brag on himself when no one else did. Called himself The Napoleon of the West. Take him as a lesson, when leaders feel the need to brag on themselves, find another leader. After the Alamo and Goliad, he thought Texas was finished. So instead of movin' his men slow and steady, he split 'em. Sent **General Urrea** and a few others down toward the coast to chase ghosts, while he took the main body north in pursuit of Houston. It was a mistake big enough to lose an empire."

The boy looked up. "Why'd he do it?"

"Pride, the kind that borders on sin," the old man said. "And the kind that don't listen to weather or wisdom. He wanted to catch Houston and finish the job himself, end the rebellion with his own hands. He didn't see that the land was already against him."

He nodded toward the dark beyond the pasture.

"The rivers were high that spring. The rains had turned every creek into a bog and every trail into a trap. Houston used it. He kept pullin' east till he hit the **Brazos River**, then stopped at a place called **Groce's Landing**. He crossed his men in small boats, one group at a time, and ordered the bridges behind him burned. Santa Anna's army came up the west bank and found nothin' but smoke and mud."

The old man's eyes narrowed as though he could still see it.

"Houston waited there near two weeks. Drilled the men, trained 'em till they could march in line without trippin' each other. He brought in cannon, shot, and powder from the coast. A man named **Henry Karnes** scouted the trails ahead, and **Deaf Smith**, half blind and twice as dangerous, kept watch on the enemy. They were a ragged bunch, but they were learnin' fast."

He took a slow draw from his pipe and let it out in a sigh.

"When Houston finally moved again, he turned south instead of east. That's when folks started to understand. He wasn't runnin' anymore. He was huntin'."

The boy grinned. "Was Santa Anna still followin'?"

"He was," the old man said. "But by then, he'd stretched his line thin as thread. His men were marchin' in small detachments, spread over miles of country. He left his supplies far behind, and the folks who might've helped him were hidin' in the woods or already gone. The land swallowed his scouts and chewed up his horses. Still, he kept comin'."

He set the cup down and folded his hands.

"Houston crossed the **Trinity River** and headed toward **Buffalo Bayou**. He was watchin' the ground more than the sky. He knew if he could find a place where the river cut one side and the marsh held the other, he could trap Santa Anna the same way Urrea had trapped Fannin.

The difference was, Houston planned to finish what he started."

The old man gave a slight nod.

"By mid-April, Santa Anna had maybe twelve hundred men left with him. Houston had near nine hundred. Not much of a gap, but enough to matter if he picked the right ground. He found it where the **San Jacinto River** met the bay. Low country, thick grass, one narrow trail in and out. That's where he stopped. The soldiers grumbled till they saw him smile. Then they knew the wait was over."

He took another sip of coffee, voice gone quiet again.

"Santa Anna made camp not far away, thinkin' he'd cornered Houston at last. What he didn't know was that Houston had been waitin' on him the whole time. The trap was set, and the land itself was helpin' spring it."

He turned to the boy.

"That's the thing about Texas. She don't pick sides, but she remembers who listens to her. Houston did. Santa Anna didn't."

The boy nodded, eyes wide.

"So this is where the war turns?"

The old man smiled faintly.

"It is. But before that turn, there was still fear and hunger, and folks didn't know yet they were marchin' toward victory. They thought they were marchin' toward the end."

He tapped the bowl of his pipe on the rail.

"We'll get to the fight soon enough. But first, you ought to know what it felt like when the world thought Texas was dyin' and didn't realize she was just drawin' breath."

The Spirit of a Broken People

The old man knocked the ashes from his pipe and sat for a while before speaking.

"By the time Houston reached the lower country," he said, "Texas was down to bone and breath. The farms were burned, the people scattered, and what passed for an army was hungry enough to eat the bark off a tree. But somehow, the spark was still there."

He leaned forward, elbows on his knees as he looked the boy in the eye.

"Along the trails east of the Brazos, folks kept movin' but stopped lookin' behind 'em. They'd lost too much for fear to matter anymore. The wagons creaked, the oxen stumbled, and still the people walked. You'd see a woman leadin' a child with one hand and pullin' a cow with the other, and she wouldn't stop till the sun did. They were done runnin'; they just hadn't realized it yet."

He nodded at at the boy.

"That's when Texas stopped bein' a place on a map and started bein' somethin' folks carried inside 'em. They'd lost homes, crops, kin, but they still had grit. You can't whip a people who don't know they're licked."

He rubbed his palms together slowly.

"Houston saw it. He saw it in the way the soldiers kept marchin' barefoot and still joked about the mud. In the way the women along the road gave up their last biscuit without a word. He wrote that the army was half-starved and half-naked, but that they'd follow him anywhere if he promised to fight. So he did."

The story widened out.

"Word spread that Houston was turnin' south, toward the coast. Men joined him out of the pine woods and the river bottoms, farmers, blacksmiths, boys too young to shave. They carried old muskets, squirrel rifles, and a handful of cannon that the mules could barely drag. They called themselves soldiers, but mostly they were Texans who'd had enough of losin'."

The old man's voice softened.

"On the nineteenth of April, they crossed Buffalo Bayou. The ground there was soft, the grass high, and the smell of the sea drifted in with the wind. Houston rode along the line and told the men they'd camp for the night. No speech, no promises. Just that quiet tone a man uses when he's made up his mind. The soldiers looked at one another and knew the run was over."

He sat back and let the chair creak.

"Out across the marsh, Santa Anna's campfires flickered like stars on the ground. He'd caught up with the Texans at last or thought he had. His men played cards and laughed; sure, the rebels would try to slip away before dawn. Houston's men sharpened knives and checked their powder horns."

The boy's voice was barely a whisper. "Did they know what was comin'?"

The old man smiled faintly.

"They knew enough. You can always tell when a man's carryin' a full heart. There was no talk of losin', only of finishin'. They'd buried their fear back on the Brazos."

He poured the last of the coffee and swirled it in the cup.

"People think San Jacinto was won in eighteen minutes. It wasn't. It was won on the road before it, in the mud, the rain, and the hunger. It was won by women who wouldn't quit and men who kept marchin' when they had nothin' left to march for. That's the spirit of Texas. It's born in the losin' and grows up in the standin'."

He looked at the boy, eyes steady.

"Next night we'll talk about the fight itself, the field by the bayou, the shout that carried from one end of the line to the other, and how eighteen minutes made a country. But remember this part, son. The courage folks talk about at San Jacinto started here, when everything looked broke and nobody gave up anyway."

He leaned back, the ancient old chair groaning under his weight.

"Sometimes," he said, "the bravest thing a man can do is keep walkin' toward the noise."

Chapter Five

The Gamble at San Jacinto.

The old man leaned back in his chair and listened to the frogs down by the creek. Their calls rose and fell like breathing. The night was soft, but the story he carried wasn't.

"Most folks think San Jacinto was all noise," he said. "Cannon fire, horses screamin', men shoutin'. Truth is, it started in silence. The kind that makes your skin crawl."

He drew on his pipe, the glow lighting his face for a moment.

"By the time Sam Houston set camp near the bayou, his men were worn to the bone. They'd marched through rain and mud, crossed half the state, and buried the last of their fear somewhere on the trail. When they stopped, they didn't know they'd picked the ground that would make a country. They just knew they were tired of runnin'."

He rocked forward, the chair creaking.

"The place wasn't much to look at. Flat, low ground where the **San Jacinto River** met **Buffalo Bayou**. One side was swamp, the other thick grass and oak trees. The air smelled of salt and wet earth. You could see the tracks of Santa Anna's army only a few miles off. Between the two camps lay a stretch of marsh, the kind that swallows sound. You'd never guess the world was about to split open there."

He let the pipe rest in his hand.

"Houston's men pitched camp near the water. Built fires that smoked more than they burned. The powder was damp, the rations near gone, but the talk that night had a different sound. They weren't mutterin' anymore. They were waitin'. Some sharpened knives, some patched boots, some just stared out across the dark. A few prayed. Mostly, they kept quiet."

The boy shifted on the step. "They knew Santa Anna was close?"

"Oh, they knew," the old man said. "Scouts had seen his flags. Houston figured he'd draw him in, let the general think he had the upper hand. Santa Anna liked easy victories. He didn't know he was walkin' into the hardest one of his life."

The wind came up, rustling the leaves. The old man's eyes followed it, far past the edge of the yard.

"I've stood out there," he said. "Grass up to your waist, sky wide enough to lose yourself in. Even now, you can feel it, that hush before somethin' big breaks loose. The ground remembers. Always does."

He poured coffee from the pot that sat cooling beside him and took a slow sip.

"Next mornin', Houston would play a gamble most men wouldn't dare. He'd trust the land, the light, and a handful of worn-out soldiers to do what nobody thought possible. But before we get to the shout and the smoke, you need to know what kind of man waits for the right moment instead of chasin' it."

He tapped the rail with his finger, a faint rhythm in the dark.

"Let's walk into that camp, boy , see Houston by the fire, studyin' the map, hear the frogs in the marsh, and the breath of an army that doesn't yet know it's about to stop runnin'. That's where the story turns."

Houston's Waiting Game

The old man rocked forward, the light from the lantern catching the smoke that drifted up from his pipe.

"Houston was a man who could wait," he said. "Most leaders want noise and movement so folks will think they're earnin' their keep. Houston didn't care about that. He was watchin' the ground, listenin' to the wind, waitin' for it to turn in his favor."

He took a sip of coffee and let it rest in his mouth before swallowing and speaking again.

"The army camped along **Buffalo Bayou**, nine hundred men if you counted generous like. They built fires from damp wood, dried their powder, and slept in the mud. Some had no boots left, others no coats. They were a mix of every kind, Tennesseans, Kentuckians, Germans, Tejanos, and boys too young for whiskers. They were half-starved, half-wild, and more dangerous for it."

He knocked the ash from his pipe against the porch rail.

"Houston spent his days ridin' the line, checkin' the posts, keepin' the men busy so they wouldn't have time to lose their nerve. He told them to clean their rifles, stack their powder dry, and wait. They didn't much like that order. After all the runnin' from the Brazos, they wanted to fight."

The boy frowned. "Why didn't he attack?"

"Because he wasn't ready," the old man said. "And because Santa Anna was doin' exactly what Houston needed him to, splittin' his forces thin and marchin' blind."

He leaned back, eyes on the dark.

"Santa Anna had near twelve hundred men when he rode up. He figured Houston would keep runnin'. Instead, he found an army camped across the bayou and too quiet for his likin'. His officers warned him not to make camp so close, but pride's a deaf commander. He ordered his men to rest, certain he'd finish the job come daylight."

The story shifted to the land itself.

"Between the two camps lay a marsh thick with reeds. Houston knew that the swamp would muffle sound and hide his movements. He sent **Deaf Smith** and **Henry Karnes** to scout the trails. That night, Deaf rode out and blew up **Vince's Bridge**, the only road Santa Anna had for retreat. When the blast echoed back across the bayou, Houston smiled for the first time in weeks."

The old man gave a slight grin of his own.

"Some called him cautious, others a coward. Truth is, he was listenin' to the land same as always. He knew the soil under his boots better than Santa Anna ever would. The river curved to guard his flank, the marsh hemmed the other side, and the enemy's back was to the water. That's what he'd been waitin' for."

He paused, letting the frogs fill the silence.

"On the mornin' of April twenty-first, the men were restless. Some cleaned their guns twice, some prayed. A few played cards on their saddles, tryin' not to think about what was comin': Houston walked the line, speakin' to each company in turn. No big speech, just words to let 'em know he was with 'em."

The boy asked, "Did he know he'd win?"

The old man smiled faintly.

"He knew he might. That was enough. He told his officers, 'We'll attack this afternoon.' They stared at him like he'd lost his mind. You don't go rushin' an army twice your size across open ground, not unless you mean to end somethin'. Houston meant to end it."

He drew on his pipe, ember flaring. "At four in the afternoon, he gave the order. The Texans formed up in three lines, **Sidney Sherman** on the left, **Edward Burleson** on the right, **Henry Millard** in the center. Behind 'em waited **Mirabeau B. Lamar's** horsemen, ready to sweep the flank. Houston rode down the front, hat in hand, tellin' the men to hold their fire till they were close enough to see the whites of the enemy's eyes."

The old man chuckled, low in his throat.

"That's the kind of man he was. Spent weeks runnin', then chose to charge broad daylight into the heart of an army that didn't even know he was comin'. He said later it was the only time he'd ever seen fortune look him in the eye."

He turned to the boy.

"Every war has one moment that decides it. This was ours. The waitin' was done. The land had gone quiet as a held breath, and Houston was ready to let it go."

His voice rose, and the old chair stopped its rocking motion as he said. "Next came the shout, the smoke, and eighteen minutes that carved Texas out of the mud."

The Battle of San Jacinto

The old man drew a slow breath before he began again.

"April twenty-first, eighteen thirty-six," he said softly. "Late afternoon. The sky was clear, the air thick with the smell of marsh grass and gun oil. Houston's men had been waitin' all day, sweatin' through their coats, listenin' to the enemy laugh across the field. The order came sudden like. 'Forward.' That one word turned nine hundred tired men into a storm."

He looked at the boy, an excitement in his eyes.

"They moved through the tall grass without a drum or bugle. Houston rode ahead on his horse, Saracen. He'd told the men not to fire till they were close. And when they came close, they let go of every ounce of rage they'd been holdin' since the Alamo and Goliad."

The old man's eyes narrowed as he remembered.

"They shouted, 'Remember the Alamo! Remember Goliad!' — two words that carried every grave in Texas with them. The sound rolled across the field like thunder. The Mexican camp went to pieces before the first volley hit. Santa Anna's men had stacked their guns, thinkin' the Texans were too tired to fight. They never had a chance."

He took a sip of coffee, his hand steady.

"The first shots came from the center, the **Twin Sisters** cannon barkin' smoke and flame. **Sidney Sherman** drove the left wing forward through the grass. **Burleson** held the right. **Henry Millard** and his men went straight into the teeth of the camp, bayonets out. **Deaf Smith**, who'd blown Vince's Bridge that mornin', rode among them, his voice carryin' above the noise."

He paused, voice roughening a little.

"You got to understand somethin', boy. These weren't soldiers trained for parade grounds. They were farmers, blacksmiths, and hunters. They'd lost friends at the Alamo and heard about their kin burned at Goliad. When they hit that line, they weren't just fightin' for Texas, they were settlin' a debt."

The field erupted. Smoke turned the air gray, and the grass caught fire where the powder flashed. The Mexican drummers tried to rally their men, beating the **Deguello**, the same tune that had meant no quarter at the Alamo. But the sound only fed the fury. The Texans answered it with lead.

The old man knocked the ashes from his pipe.

"They didn't stop when the Mexicans turned and ran. They chased 'em into the swamp along **Buffalo Bayou**, gunnin' down men who threw up their hands. Houston tried to call 'em back, but no one could hear him. The noise was too much, and vengeance had been waitin' too long. Some dropped their guns and used the butts as clubs. Others fired till their barrels smoked red. It wasn't a battle anymore. It was every hurt from the last month poured out in one breath."

He looked at the boy, voice softer now.

"Houston said later he tried to stop the killin'. Maybe he did. Maybe no man could've. He took a ball through the ankle, but he stayed on his horse, shoutin' for order.

The men didn't listen till the swamp itself stopped their run. They'd come to the end of the ground."

He lit his pipe again, the flame flickering.

"The fight lasted eighteen minutes, give or take. Eighteen minutes that broke one army and built a country. Six hundred Mexicans dead, two hundred wounded, and seven hundred taken prisoner. The Texans lost nine. Nine, boy. The whole war turned in less time than it takes to boil coffee."

He drew a long breath and let it out.

"When the smoke cleared, the field was quiet. Horses wandered through the grass, and the smell of powder hung low. The men looked around like they'd woken from a dream. Some sat down and cried. Others just stared at their hands, not sure what they'd done or what it meant. That's what victory looks like when you're close enough to smell it, relief and a little shame."

He looked toward the dark beyond the porch.

"The bayou still runs past that field. I've stood there, watched the reeds bend with the wind. Folks built cities and roads since then, but the place don't forget. You stand quiet, and you can still hear the echo of those shouts, that mix of anger and freedom. It's a sound that don't die easy."

The boy whispered, "Eighteen minutes?"

"Eighteen," the old man said. "But the rage that fueled it had been buildin' for months. The Alamo, Goliad, the runnin', the fear, all of it came due that day. Houston may have planned the battle, but every man on that field fought his own war."

He leaned back, the rocker creaking.

"That's why San Jacinto matters. Not because it was glorious, but because it was human. Every sin, every sorrow, every bit of stubborn pride Texas ever carried came to a head in that swamp. When it was over, the world turned quiet, and the flag that rose above the smoke wasn't just cloth, it was the price paid in full."

The Capture of Santa Anna

The old man sat quietly for a while before speaking, the sound of the night seeping in around him.

"When the guns went still, Texas was born," he said. "But what came next would decide what kind of country it was gonna be."

He leaned forward, elbows on his knees, pipe forgotten in his hand as he drew the boy in, toward his story, towards that day in April.

"The next mornin' was thick with fog. The ground was soft, the air heavy with the smell of powder and blood. Houston's men walked through the smoke, checkin' for the livin'. Some of the Mexican soldiers were lyin' face down in the mud, hands open. Others were wanderin' without rifles, lost and stunned. The ones who could still stand were gathered and held under guard."

He paused, lookin' toward the pasture as if he could see it.

"Out there on that wet ground, you could feel it , the anger drainin' out and somethin' quieter takin' its place. The men were tired, their rage spent. Houston himself was on the ground, his boot off, blood soakin' through a bandage on his ankle. He'd been hit by a musket ball that shattered the bone. They carried him to a tree and sat him down. From there, he gave what orders he could. His voice was steady, but it carried a weight that wasn't just pain."

He took a slow draw of his pipe, the ember flaring.

"By midday, the search parties were comin' back. They brought in prisoners, supplies, wagons, anything that still moved. Around mid-afternoon, a patrol led by **Joel Robison** and **James Sylvester** came ridin' in with a man they'd pulled from the marsh. He was wearin' a private's coat, filthy and wet, face streaked with mud. At first, nobody paid him any mind. Then one of the captured officers spotted him and shouted, 'El Presidente!'"

The old man grinned.

"That's how they found **Santa Anna**, hidin' in plain sight. The man who'd promised no mercy at the Alamo, who'd ordered the killin' at Goliad, was standin' there shakin' in his boots. They brought him before Houston, who was leanin' against that same tree, pale and hurt but still in charge."

The boy frowned. "Did they hang him?"

"They could've," the old man said. "Plenty wanted to. There was enough hate in that camp to fill the river. But

Houston looked at him for a long time and said, 'We've had enough killin.' Then he ordered the men to lower their guns."

He let the quiet sit for a moment before going on.

Santa Anna offered to trade his life for peace. Said he'd order the rest of his troops to leave Texas. Some of the men called it a trick. Houston told 'em, 'Maybe so, but I'd rather deal with a livin' liar than a dead martyr.' So he spared him. Signed papers that ended the fight. The Republic of Texas was a fact before the ink was dry."

He turned back toward the boy, voice softer now.

"That was the difference between Houston and the rest. The men at San Jacinto fought with rage; Houston won with restraint. He knew you can't build a country on vengeance. You can win a war that way, sure, but not a future."

The old man poured the last of the coffee into his cup, the sound small in the dark.

"I've stood on that field, boy. The grass still grows high, the bayou still winds slow. They say you can hear the frogs at night same as back then. If you stand quiet, you'll catch it, not the sound of war, but of somethin' new bein' born."

He leaned back as he wiped his face with his sleeve, the chair creaking under his weight.

"Most folks think victory's about who falls. It ain't. It's about who stands after. Houston stood that day, not just for Texas but for what Texas could be, a place big enough to hold mercy and still call itself strong."

The boy was silent, looking out into the dark.

After a moment, the old man said, "That's the last lesson of the Revolution, son. A man can carry fury only so far. After that, he's gotta decide what kind of peace he wants to live with."

"Eighteen Minutes and Forever"

The old man's pipe had gone cold again. He didn't bother to light it this time. He just looked out across the dark pasture where a thin mist lay close to the ground.

"Eighteen minutes," he said softly. "That's how long the fight lasted. Eighteen minutes to win a country, but it took years to pay for it."

He stared at his cup, running his fingers over its aged handle and his craggy face glanced towards the mist. He put the cup by his chair and took his pipe from the old rock that served as its resting place.

"People talk about the glory of San Jacinto, the banners, the shouts, the songs. But the truth is quieter. Those men were too tired to cheer. They sat in the mud, bleedin' and breathin', tryin' to understand what they'd done. They didn't see history that day, just the end of runnin'."

He looked at the boy.

"Texas came out of those eighteen minutes. It was born in noise and smoke, and it grew up fast. Some folks found hope in it; others just found another kind of work. Freedom's never clean, boy. It's earned, not given, and it comes with a long shadow."

He knocked the pipe against his boot and watched the last bit of ash fall through the boards.

"The war was over, but the reckonin' had only just begun. The farmers in the east went back to plowin', the widows to prayin', and the Tejanos, the ones who'd fought beside us, started lookin' over their shoulders. The enslaved were still in chains, though they'd heard talk of liberty and wondered when it might reach them. Every man in Texas got somethin' out of victory, but not everyone got the same thing."

He rose slowly, stretching the stiffness from his back.

"That's the next part of it, boy. What victory gave and what it took away. The Republic that came after, proud, broke, and fightin' itself as much as anyone else."

He picked up the coffeepot, refilling his cup with its dregs, and smiled faintly.

"Eighteen minutes made Texas. The rest of her story is about learnin' how to live with it."

He looked out over the fields one more time.

"Next time we'll talk about that new country, what freedom meant for the settlers, the soldiers, the Tejanos, and the enslaved. A land proud enough to stand on its own legs, but still figurin' out what kind of heart it had."

The chair creaked once more, and the night closed back in around them.

CHAPTER SIX

The Republic of Texas: Between Dreams and Debts

"The Price of Freedom"

The old man sat quiet for a spell, the pipe in his hand gone cold again. He looked out toward the pasture, where a light fog had rolled in low and gray across the grass. "Winnin' a country's the easy part," he said. "Keepin' it honest, that's the work that comes after."

"When the fight at San Jacinto ended, Texas was free, or thought she was. Houston's army limped away from the field, men shoutin' and laughin', some cryin' because they'd lived to see another sunrise. Behind 'em, the dead from the battle lay quiet in the mud. It was victory all right, but it didn't look much like the pictures folks paint later."

He drew a slow breath and continued. "Word spread quick. Families still on the road in the **Runaway Scrape** stopped their wagons when riders came hollerin' that Santa Anna had been whipped and caught alive. Some fell to their knees and prayed. Others just stared, not believin' yet. A few cried for the men who weren't comin' back to see it. The war had been short, but it burned hot, and it left the ground scorched clear through."

The old man's eyes stayed on the horizon for a long moment before he answered.

"Better for some," he said. "For others, it just got harder. That's the way of things."

He drew his boot heel across the porch plank, leaving a pale line of dust.

"The farmers out east went back to what they knew. They mended fences, patched their roofs, and planted fresh rows of corn. The soldiers who made it home walked in with their boots worn through and their rifles more rust than iron. They were thin, proud, and dead tired, but they'd done what they set out to do."

The boy said, "So everything was better then?"

The old man smiled faintly, eyes still on the dark horizon. "Better for some. Harder for others. That's the way it goes. "The ones out east went back to what was left," he said. "They mended fences, patched the leaks, turned the dirt over again for corn. The soldiers who made it home walked in barefoot, rifles pitted with rust, bellies near empty. There wasn't any pay waitin', just a handshake and a flag someone had sewn from a scrap of dress cloth.

Pride don't fill a man long, but it'll keep him standin' for a spell."

He struck a match and coaxed the pipe back to life, the flame flickering' against his face.

"Houston went back to San Antonio that summer," he said. "Rode slow, favorin' the bad leg. Folks were callin' him a hero by then, though he never took to the word. Said heroes were for poems, not politics. He'd helped win a country, sure enough, but it was broke the day it was born. The treasury held more dust than coin, and the money they printed wasn't worth the ink on it." Still, there was a new flag flyin' over the old presidio, a single star on a field of red, white, and blue. Folks looked up at it and believed for a while."

He exhaled smoke, the ember glowin' bright in the dark. "Texas called herself a republic, but she was really just a handful of towns and a lot of promises. The land was wide, the people few, and the debts already heavy. But nobody talked about money then. They talked about freedom. Every man who'd carried a musket thought he'd earned a piece of it. Some got it. Some didn't."

He looked down at his hands. "Houston was elected president that fall. The first thing he said was that peace was better than glory. The second thing he said was that the country was broke. He tried to talk about taxes and trade, but nobody wanted to hear it. They wanted to celebrate. Folks threw dances in Galvez Town, parades in

Columbia. They'd waited a long time to call this place their own, and they weren't gonna let the numbers spoil it."

He smiled faintly, shaking his head. "Freedom feels lighter when you don't count the cost. But the bills always come due, one way or another."

The boy leaned forward. "Did they know it wouldn't last?"

The old man looked at him for a long moment before answering. "Some did. Houston knew, a few others. But most were just tired of losin'. They figured anything was better than takin' orders from Mexico. They didn't see that they'd traded one kind of dependin' for another. A country's like a man, boy, the first thing he does after winnin' a fight is usually the thing that costs him most later."

He took another puff from his pipe, the smoke driftin' into the soft night air. "Texas was proud, poor, and stubborn as a mule. The fight had made her free, but she hadn't yet figured out what to do with that freedom. That's what the next years were about, learnin' to live with what victory gave her."

He looked off into the dark pasture where the stars were coming' out one by one. "Next part of the story's about the livin', the farmers, the soldiers, the Tejanos, the folks who worked this ground after the guns went quiet. The war made heroes. The Republic made people. And that's where we'll start."

The Settlers and the Soil

The old man shifted his boots against the porch rail and watched a moth drift through the lamplight.

"When the fightin' was done," he said, "the land was all most folks had left to believe in. The rivers hadn't changed, and the dirt didn't care who claimed it. So they went back to it."

He drew on his pipe and waved the smoke away with his hat brim.

"The settlers in the east took up the plow again. They cleared brush from the bottoms along the Trinity and Neches, planted corn where the weeds had gone to seed. Families built cabins from pine cut that same day, roofed with split shakes that leaked when the rain came sideways. It wasn't pretty, but it was theirs."

He looked over at the boy.

"You'd hear hammers and saws from daylight to dark, every nail cost near what a man made in a week, so most used wooden pegs. Neighbors traded labor more than money. If a man raised a cabin, the next day he'd be raisin' somebody else's. That's how towns like **Nacogdoches**, **Huntsville**, and **Washington-on-the-Brazos** started, a few roofs, a blacksmith, a store with more promises than stock."

He chuckled softly.

"Paper money was the joke of the day. Fancy looking bills and the backs had a big star printed in red ink, called 'em redbacks. The Republic printed it faster than it could count it. Folks said if you stacked every bill in Austin, you could climb clear to heaven, but you'd starve before you got there. A man might take payment for a cow, but by the time he got home, the paper was worth less than the rope tied to it. Now that was probably an exaggeration, but that is what the money had become, a joke."

The chair creaked as he leaned back.

"Still, land was cheap, four cents an acre if you could pay the fees, free if you were willin' to defend it. That drew more folks than any poster or preacher ever did. Wagons rolled in from Arkansas, Louisiana, and Tennessee. Some were dreamers, some drifters, some runnin' from debts or sheriffs. All of 'em said the same thing: 'Texas is a new start.'"

The boy asked, "Was it?"

"For some," the old man said. "The soil in the east was kind, black as coffee grounds, and near bottomless. Crops came easy. A good rain and a little sweat could make a man feel rich. But west of the Brazos, the ground turned mean again, chalky, dry, and full of mesquite roots. A few settlers tried anyway. Most packed up and went back east before the first winter."

He lifted the coffeepot, found it empty, and set it down again.

"Houston tried to keep the peace while the country found its feet. He opened trade with the States, sent men to talk to Mexico about drawin' a real border. He said schools were the measure of a free land and called for buildin' a few, though there wasn't money for chalk, let alone books. His biggest task was keepin' the army from turnin' into a gang of politicians with rifles."

He smiled a little at the thought.

"Then came **Mirabeau B. Lamar**, the second president. Now there was a man who thought big, new capital at **Austin**, fancy buildings, a navy, and talk about stretchin' the Republic clear to the Pacific. He believed in education and spent what little we had to prove it. Trouble was, dreams cost, and Texas didn't have two nickels to rub together. By the end of his term, the debt was near seven million dollars, more zeroes than the treasury could count."

The Old Man rested his hat on his knee.

"Out in the country, folks hardly noticed presidents unless taxes came due. What they saw was fences goin' up, cotton sproutin' white, and herds of cattle driftin' toward the coast. The east turned into a patchwork of small farms and big plantations. Corn for the poor, cotton for the rich, cattle for everybody. Every wagon road turned into a trail of dust and promise."

He looked toward the dark trees.

"Most lived lean but proud. They held barn dances, sang hymns under brush arbors, and swapped stories till the candles burned down. Sundays, you'd see wagons lined up outside a clapboard church, women in homespun dresses, men in shirts gone gray from work. They'd pray, eat, and talk about the new country like it was kin."

He rubbed his hands together slowly.

"But it wasn't all peace. The debts kept growin', and the paper money kept fallin'. Ranchers fought over brands, farmers over water. Out west, raids still came down from the plains. The Rangers rode near every month, tryin' to hold a line that never stayed put. The land was rich, but the Republic was broke, a grand idea payin' rent on reality."

He smiled faintly.

"I remember my granddaddy sayin' the best thing about those years was the stories. Every campfire had a hero in it, every porch a politician. Folks could argue about anythin', which river was widest, which general smartest, which whiskey cleanest. They didn't have much, but they had pride enough to share."

The boy said, "Did people still believe in Texas?"

"Oh, they believed," the old man said. "Belief's cheap, and it keeps a man warm. The settlers called this place God's country even when the rain didn't come. They'd stand on the porch lookin' at a field gone to dust and still say tomorrow would be better. That's the thing about Texans, boy. They mistake stubbornness for faith, and half the time it works."

He laughed softly, the sound low in his throat.

"The Republic was young, wild, and in debt. But it was alive. You could feel it in the ground when you walked, a hum, like the land itself was stretchin' awake after a long sleep. Houston wanted peace, Lamar wanted glory, and the farmers just wanted rain. None of 'em got exactly what they asked for, but they kept tryin'."

He knocked his pipe empty and looked out toward the far trees.

"That was Texas in the first years, half dream, half dust, all heart. We thought we'd found paradise, and in a way, we had. We just didn't know yet what paradise costs."

Chains That Stayed: Slavery in the Republic

The old man ran his thumb along the cool rim of his coffee cup before speaking.

"Now, folks like to say the Revolution was fought for freedom," he said. "And maybe it was, for some. But freedom don't weigh the same for everybody. Texas learned that early."

He drew a breath and set the cup down.

"When we became a republic, the men who wrote the laws made sure one thing didn't change: the right to own another person. The Constitution of the Republic protected slavery clear as day. Said no slave could be freed without permission from Congress, and any free Negro who stayed in the country too long could be run out or sold back into bondage. That was written in ink while the blood of the war was still fresh."

He shook his head slowly.

"The same men who'd stood on the field at San Jacinto talkin' about liberty went home to plantations with folks workin' under a whip. They said it was the way of the South, the price of cotton, the will of God, any excuse that sounded noble. Truth is, it was money. Cotton and sugar kept the country floatin', and both were built on backs that didn't have a say."

He tapped his pipe against the rail, but didn't light it again.

"By the early forties, near thirty thousand enslaved people lived here, most in the bottomlands east of the Brazos. Every wagon comin' from the States brought more, planters movin' west with their families, their tools, and their chains. They called it progress. The land called it somethin' else."

The boy spoke carefully. "Did anyone fight it?"

The old man nodded.

"A few. **José Navarro**, one of the Tejanos who helped write the laws, argued that freedom ought to mean what it says. Some preachers tried to remind folks about their Bibles. But words didn't travel far. The ones with the land had the power, and the ones in chains didn't have a voice to carry theirs."

He rubbed the back of his neck as though trying to work out an old ache.

"I remember an old preacher tellin' my granddaddy, 'The Lord freed the land, but not the hands that tilled it.' That line stuck. It meant the war had set Texas loose from Mexico but left a whole people in the same bind. The country liked to talk about liberty; it just didn't want to pay the price of it."

The porch fell quiet. Out in the dark, a whip-poor-will called once and was still again.

"Some of the enslaved ran," the old man went on. "They headed south toward Mexico, where slavery had been outlawed. It was near two hundred miles of hard country, brush, rivers, heat, but a few made it. The rest were hunted down and dragged back. Rangers called it keepin' the peace; and the planters called it protectin' property. Either way, the chains stayed."

He looked at the boy.

"Freedom's a word folks use easy. Hard part's lettin' it belong to everybody. Texas was still learnin' that, and we still are, same as the rest of the world."

He leaned back, chair creaking.

"By the time Houston came back into office in '42, he saw what was happenin'. He said the country couldn't last long if it stayed part slave and part free, but even he couldn't untie that knot. The cotton was too good, the markets too hungry. So he tried to keep peace with Mexico instead, said war cost money we didn't have. The planters called him soft for it. But he wasn't wrong."

He looked toward the stars barely visible through the haze.

"I reckon every country's got a shadow. For Texas, it was slavery. It fed the farms and poisoned the soul at the same time. Folks didn't want to see it, but it was there, in the songs sung in the fields, in the markets, in the quiet between the verses of every hymn."

He rubbed the arm of his chair with a calloused hand.

"That's why I say freedom came slow here. The papers said we were independent, but the truth of it was chained up in the cotton rows. It would take another war, and another generation, before the word meant what it should."

The boy's voice was quiet. "Did they ever fix it?"

The old man shook his head.

"Some wrongs don't get fixed, boy. They get carried till they wear down, like river stones. We're still carryin' that one."

He leaned forward, poured what was left of the coffee into his cup, and stared into it for a long time before he spoke again.

"The next part of the story ain't about the rich or the generals. It's about the ones who fought beside us and got pushed aside after, the **Tejanos**, the friends who helped build the Republic and paid for it with their homes."

Forgotten Allies: The Tejanos and the Cost of Distrust

The old man's hands rested on his knees, the firelight showing the cracks in his knuckles.

"Now, while the settlers were buildin' and the planters were countin' cotton," he said, "another story was playin' out, one that didn't get told much. It was about the **Tejanos**, the Spanish speakin' folks who fought shoulder to shoulder with us for independence. When the smoke cleared, they were the ones left out in it."

He shifted in his chair and looked toward the dark line of trees beyond the yard.

"Men like **Juan Seguín**, **José Antonio Navarro**, and **Plácido Benavides**, they weren't just names on paper. They were Texans before Texas had a name. They scouted for Houston, fought at San Jacinto, and carried news when no one else could. Seguín commanded a company of Tejano cavalry that rode straight into the fight at the Alamo before he was sent out for help. When he came back, there wasn't anybody left to help."

He took a long breath, shaking his head.

"When the Republic stood up on its own two legs, them same men found the ground shiftin' under 'em. Folks had lost family at the Alamo and Goliad, and all they could see when they looked at a Tejano face was the enemy's uniform. The hatred for Santa Anna spread like brush fire, and it didn't stop at the border. It burned through neighbors and old friends."

The boy frowned. "Even the ones who fought for Texas?"

"Even them," the old man said. "Seguín came back to San Antonio after the war, wearin' the same uniform he'd worn at San Jacinto. Said he was proud to serve the Republic. The townsfolk whispered that he was spyin' for Mexico. Took a few months of that before they ran him clean out of town. He crossed the Rio Grande with a price on his head, exiled by the country he helped build."

He rubbed the arm of his chair, the sound rough in the quiet.

José Navarro stayed longer. He helped write the laws that made the Republic, fought for schools and justice. But even he couldn't walk through San Antonio without hearin' slurs from men who'd once shared his table. They took his land bit by bit through false claims and new surveys. That's how Texas repaid its allies, with suspicion and lawsuits."

He spat once over the rail.

"Out west, Tejano ranchers lost their herds to raids from both sides. Mexican troops still crossed the border, burnin' small towns in retaliation, and Rangers answered the same way. Folks who tried to stay neutral got caught between both fires. It wasn't much of a life, defendin' a home that belonged to a country that no longer wanted you."

The Old Man's eyes narrowed, his tone softening.

"Most Tejano families didn't leave. They just kept quiet, worked their land, and prayed the new government would settle down. Some changed their names or stopped speakin' Spanish in public. Their children learned English quick, not because they wanted to forget who they were, but because it was safer."

He looked at the boy.

"We talk about the Republic like it was one big family, but it wasn't. It was a house with rooms that didn't fit together. The Anglos had the keys, the Tejanos had the memories, and the enslaved had the work. That's the truth of it."

He reached down, picked up a pebble from the porch, and tossed it out into the dark.

"The saddest part was that Texas could've been somethin' else. The mix of Spanish, Mexican, and Anglo blood, that's what made her different. We could've built a country wide enough for all of it. But fear got the better of us. Fear and pride. Always does."

He sat back and let the night fill the silence for a while.

"**Juan Seguín** came back years later, gray-haired and tired. Said he forgave the Republic, though I reckon he never forgot it. Folks in San Antonio finally put his name on a street sign, long after it stopped matterin' to him."

He rubbed the back of his neck.

"Texas has always been two things at once, proud and forgetful. We remember the battles and the heroes. We forget the helpers, the neighbors, the ones who carried water while the flags were flyin'. Every country does it, but we do it louder."

The boy asked quietly, "Did they ever make it right?"

The old man gave a slow shake of his head.

"Not really. Some wrongs just fade into habit. The Tejanos built this place the same as anyone, and most died hopin' their kids would be treated better. Some were. Some weren't. But their names are still in the rivers and the towns. You can't wash that out, no matter how many times you repaint the map."

He lifted his cup, found it empty, and smiled at the boy.

"That's the cost of distrust, son. You win a war for independence, and sometimes you lose the people who helped you win it. Texas learned that the hard way."

He set the cup down, the sound soft in the quiet.

"Next comes the part folks don't write songs about, the years when the Republic tried to stand on its own legs and stumbled more often than it walked. But for now, it's enough to remember that freedom's only worth somethin' if it's shared."

A Country Still Growin' Up"

The old man stayed quiet for a spell. The crickets had gone still, and the air felt heavy, the way it does before daylight. He rubbed his hands together out of habit, slow and steady.

"Texas was free," he said at last. "But she couldn't sit easy. Never has." The same spirit that won her freedom kept her from sittin' still long enough to figure out what it meant. We had pride, land, and big talk, but not enough money or mercy to go with it."

He leaned back in his chair and looked at the boy.

"Every new country's a gamble. Ours was no different. We tried to run before we could walk. We built laws faster than schools and raised armies faster than churches. We made promises to God and man, but we couldn't afford to keep 'em all."

He smiled a little, tired but not bitter.

"Still, you can't say it wasn't worth the try. The Republic had its flaws, more than most, but it had heart. Folks worked hard, argued harder, and somehow kept it alive for near ten years. In the end, it joined the Union, but Texas never did lose that habit of standin' a little apart."

He picked up his hat and turned it in his hands, the brim catching the faint lantern light.

"The ones who came after us inherited both things, the courage and the contradictions. The land gave 'em both, and they're still figurin' out which to keep."

He nodded toward the east, where a thin line of gray was starting to stretch above the treetops.

"Sun's comin' up," he said. "You can see the light before you feel it, and that's how progress works, too. Texas was young back then, full of fight, full of pride, still learnin' what kind of heart it had. She's older now, but I'm not sure she's done learnin'."

The boy rose and leaned on the rail, looking out at the first hint of morning.

"What comes next?" he asked.

The old man smiled, tugging his coat a little tighter against the cool air.

"Next part's about the forts and the dust," he said. "The Rangers ridin' again, the buffalo herds movin' north, and the way the frontier kept pushin' back no matter how many fences folks built. Texas didn't rest long. She never has."

He stood, stretched his back, and nodded toward the horizon.

"Go on and get some sleep, boy. The world'll still be here when you wake. And so will the stories."

He tipped his hat and walked inside, leaving the chair to rock once more in the soft breeze, the last curl of pipe smoke drifting' out into the dawn.

CHAPTER SEVEN

The Republic Tested: Santa Fe, Mier, and the Black Beans

"The Trouble with Pride"

The night was still, and the moon sat low, wide as a coin above the trees. The old man leaned his chair back on two legs, one boot pressed against the porch post for balance. He didn't speak at first. When he did, his voice carried that low drawl of someone remembering mistakes that weren't his but felt like they could've been.

"Freedom's a fine thing," he said, "but it does strange work on men. Makes some humble, makes others reckless. After San Jacinto, Texas, had both kinds. We'd bled to win a country and near bled again tryin' to hold it."

He rocked forward, boots thudding on the planks.

"By forty-one, the Republic had a new president, Mirabeau B. Lamar, a man who could talk thunder and dream storms. He wanted Texas to be more than a strip of land between rivers. He saw empire in his sleep, stretchin' clear to the Rio Grande and up to Santa Fe. Said the land was ours by right of courage and God's blessin'. Houston, sittin' out of office by then, called it what it was, pride wearin' a hero's hat."

He reached for the coffeepot, poured himself a little, and let the steam roll up into the cool air.

"Lamar had big plans, new schools, a new navy, and a new capital he called Austin, built out there in the middle of nowhere to prove Texas didn't fear the frontier. Trouble was, all that buildin' cost money the Republic didn't have. The debt was already heavy, but pride don't check the ledger."

He rubbed his thumb along the cup's rim.

"Most folks back then wanted peace. They were plowin' fields and raisin' stock, tryin' to build somethin' they could keep. But the men in the fancy coats were still chasin' glory. Lamar said Texas was destined to control the whole of the West. He sent a party to claim Santa Fe, traders, soldiers, and dreamers, all headin' into a desert they didn't understand. That's where our trouble starts."

The boy leaned forward. "Wasn't Santa Fe in Mexico then?"

The old man nodded.

"Still was. That's what made it foolish. Houston told 'em it was suicide. Lamar said it was destiny. Folks believed the man who spoke louder. Happens more often than you'd think. You see boy, in politics most people don't want truth, they want what makes them feel good."

He took a sip of coffee and grimaced at the bitterness.

"I remember my granddaddy sayin' every country's got a year when it loses its good sense. For Texas, it was eighteen forty-one. We'd fought too hard to stay small, so we tried to grow faster than the land would let us. Called it expansion. Truth was, it was pride, and pride'll send a man ridin' into country that don't want him."

The chair creaked as he leaned back again, the lamplight flickering against his boots.

"Santa Fe was near eight hundred miles from Austin. You could die of thirst halfway there, and most did. That expedition was the Republic's first big mistake, and it wouldn't be the last. Texas had to learn the hard way that a flag don't make you wise, just visible."

He looked out into the dark, the pipe ember glowing faintly as he drew from it.

"Let's talk about that long march into the west, the dust, the heat, and the lesson the desert gave us for free. Every country's got to earn its humility sooner or later. Ours came one wagonload at a time."

The Santa Fe Expedition (1841)

The old man drew from his pipe and let the smoke drift slowly.

"Lamar's Santa Fe plan sounded grand enough when he said it," he began. "He told folks Texas would control every trail from the Gulf clear to the Rockies, that traders in New Mexico were just waitin' to fly our flag. Most people in Austin liked the sound of it. They always do, when a man promises gold instead of sweat."

He set the pipe aside and rubbed the back of his neck.

"Problem was, nobody who signed up knew what waited out there. The country between the Brazos and Santa Fe was dry as bone and mean as home spun sin. You can ride three days across the Llano Estacado and see nothin' but sky and mesquite. Water holes hide in sand and vanish when you need 'em. Lamar sent near three hundred men, merchants, soldiers, surveyors, even a newspaperman or two, followin' wagons loaded with trade goods. They left Austin in June when the heat was already thick enough to choke a mule."

The boy frowned. "Did Houston try to stop them?"

"He did," the old man said. "He called it a fool's errand. But Lamar was president then, and his pride was louder than reason. Houston stayed home and waited for the land to settle the argument."

He peered intently at the boy.

"Out past San Angelo, the grass gave way to rock and dust. Wagons broke, oxen dropped, men got lost lookin' for rivers that had gone dry years before. Some days, they marched by moonlight just to save water. They argued over maps, cursed the sun, and ate what the hunters could bring down. A few turned back before they even reached the Pecos. The rest kept movin' because no one wanted to admit the mistake."

The old man's voice softened.

"When they finally stumbled into New Mexico, half starved and wearin' rags, they found Mexican troops waitin'. Not traders, not friends, soldiers. The Texans were too worn down to fight. They laid down their arms after a short skirmish and hoped for decent treatment. They didn't get it. Urrea's men took their weapons, stripped what was worth takin', and marched 'em toward Mexico City."

He took a slow sip of coffee and kept talking.

"It was near two thousand miles from where they were caught to where they ended up. The trail wound through desert and mountain, heat and snow, and men dropped along the way. Some died of thirst, some from the lash, some just lay down and didn't get up again. By the time the survivors reached the capital, they were walkin' ghosts. Lamar's grand expedition had turned into a line of prisoners."

The boy asked quietly, "Did they ever get home?"

"Some did," the old man said. "Took near a year and a half. A few escaped and wandered back across the Rio Grande with nothin' but bones and stubbornness holdin' 'em together. When Houston came back to power, he sent wagons to fetch the rest. He said the Republic had been punished enough by its own pride."

He shook his head.

"The Santa Fe expedition cost more than any battle. We lost men, wagons, and what little respect the Republic still had abroad. Mexico laughed at us, the United States called us reckless, and the treasury was emptier than before. Lamar's dream of empire dried up with the last water hole on that trail."

The old man leaned back and looked toward the stars.

"I've ridden parts of that country," he said. "It's quiet now, just wind and mesquite. You'd never guess men once died there for a map line nobody remembers. The desert don't hold grudges, it just waits for the next fool who thinks he can master it."

He tapped the ashes from his pipe into the dust at his feet.

"Every country's got to learn the weight of its own name, boy. For Texas, that weight came heavy and early. After Santa Fe, we stopped talkin' about glory for a while and started talkin' about survival. At least till pride found another road south."

He looked over at the boy and gave a slight nod.

"That road led to San Antonio, to another march, another handful of men who thought they could outrun their luck. That's where the next part starts."

The Mexican Raids and the Somervell Expedition (1842)

The old man poured a little more coffee, though it had long gone cold.

"Santa Fe should've been lesson enough," he said. "But lessons don't take easy with men who think they've been cheated of glory. By the next year, Texas was boilin' again."

He rubbed a calloused thumb over the rim of the tin cup.

"In March of '42, the Mexicans came north under General Rafael Vásquez, near seven hundred strong. They crossed the Rio Grande, rolled through San Antonio, and raised the Mexican flag right there on the plaza. Folks woke up to the sound of drums and soldiers in the street. Vásquez didn't stay long, two days, maybe, but it was long enough to scare the whole Republic. He marched back south before Houston's army could reach him, but the damage was done."

He set the cup down and glanced toward the boy.

"News spread fast. In the east, they said the war had started again. Houston called for patience, told people not to act without orders. Texans never did take kindly to that kind of talk. Before the week was out, riders were in every town hollerin' for volunteers."

He leaned back, the chair creaking as it always did..

"That fall, it happened again. General Adrian Woll brought a thousand men across the border and took San

Antonio all over again. It was like openin' an old wound that hadn't healed right. They captured near seventy prisoners, lawyers, judges, and farmers, marched 'em off south as hostages. The people were mad clean through. This time, Houston's words couldn't hold 'em."

The old man's jaw tightened.

"Out of that anger came General Alexander Somervell and seven hundred fifty men, volunteers mostly, with no uniforms and less discipline. They rode south that winter, sayin' they'd make Mexico pay. Houston gave him orders to defend the border and come home if the fight carried too far. Somervell crossed anyway."

He paused, looking off toward the horizon as though the memory was still riding there.

"They reached Laredo first, took the town, raised the flag, then marched to Guerrero: no big battles, just hungry men in worn-out boots. When orders came down to pull back, Somervell saw the truth: the army was tired, the horses spent, and the cause had gone sideways. He told his men to head home."

The boy leaned forward. "And they listened?"

The old man shook his head.

"About half did. The rest didn't have sense enough. Near three hundred stayed behind, sayin' the war wasn't done. They picked Colonel William Fisher to lead 'em and swore they'd march to Mier, a town just inside Mexico, and make their own kind of victory. Fisher was a brave man, but he didn't have Houston's patience. He crossed that river on Christmas Eve, and with that step, Texas walked straight into its darkest chapter." "That's where the next mistake waited, on the far bank."

He took a draw from his pipe and blew the smoke toward the night sky.

The Mier Expedition and the Black Bean Affair

The old man turned the cup in his hands a few times before he spoke.

"When Fisher and his men crossed the Rio Grande that Christmas Eve, they figured they'd find honor waitin' on the other side," he said. "What they found was hunger, cold, and a whole army that knew the ground better than they ever would."

He drew a slow breath.

"They hit the town of Mier at daybreak on the twenty-fifth of December 1842. The plan was quick and simple, take the place, gather supplies, and head back across the river before the main Mexican force could reach 'em. But nothin' in war stays simple for long. Fisher's scouts were late, the locals were ready, and by the time the Texans pushed into town, the streets were full of soldiers. Windows and rooftops flashed with musket fire, and the air went thick with powder smoke."

He leaned back and rubbed his jaw.

"They fought house to house for near a full day. The Texans were outnumbered five to one, but they had grit.

Every doorway was a fort, every rooftop a fight. Late that night, out of water and down to the last of their powder, they tried to bargain. The Mexicans promised they'd be treated fair if they gave up. Fisher believed it, or maybe he just didn't want to watch more men die. He surrendered his sword, and that was that."

He looked at the boy, voice low.

"Next mornin' they were tied in pairs and marched south. It was supposed to be to Matamoros, but the orders kept changin'. Santa Anna wanted prisoners he could parade. The guards wanted revenge. The trail turned cruel quick. They walked barefoot, bellies empty, through cactus and heat by day, and cold that cut bone by night. Men fell out every few miles and didn't get back up."

He paused and reached for the coffeepot, pouring the last of it into his cup.

"Near the town of Salado, some of the Texans decided they'd had enough. They jumped the guards and broke for the brush. About two hundred made a run for it. A few found the river and slipped away, but most got turned around in the desert. The sun killed more than the bullets did. They wandered for days till the cavalry caught 'em. Fisher was still with 'em when they were dragged back to the column. He said nothin'. Didn't need to."

The old man's hand hovered over the pipe, but didn't lift it.

"When they reached Saltillo, Santa Anna's orders were waitin'. He wanted every tenth man shot to make sure the rest remembered who ruled the border. The guards filled a jar with beans, a hundred and fifty-nine white, seventeen black. Each prisoner was made to draw. If you pulled a white bean, you lived. If you pulled a black one, you died."

He let the words hang there for a moment, the night around him gone still.

"The first to draw was a boy from Georgia, no older than you. He pulled white, laughed, and fainted dead away. The second man pulled black. He nodded once, said, 'Tell my folks,' and stepped aside. They say not one man cried or begged. The draw went on till the jar was empty. Seventeen men stood in a line and met their end before sundown. The rest were marched away in chains."

The boy's voice was quiet. "What happened to the others?"

"Prison," the old man said. "Months of it. Some got sick, some got mean, some just stopped talkin'. When Houston came back to power, he begged Mexico for their release. A few were freed in '44, thin as fence posts and half blind from the march. They came home to farms gone and families moved on. The war had taken years they didn't have to spare."

He stared off toward the trees, his voice gone softer.

"The Republic learned somethin' from Mier, though most folks pretended not to. Pride can win you a moment, but it won't keep you alive. We'd tried to turn revenge into victory twice, and both times it near killed us. After that, Houston said no more adventures across the border. He meant it. Texas had finally run out of heroes and excuses."

He rubbed the arm of his chair with slow circles of his thumb.

"I've been to Mier, long years later. The town's quiet now. The river runs slow, and there's a small stone marker where the fight took place. Folks there don't talk about the war much. Maybe they remember the same as we do, that nothin' lasts longer than a mistake paid in blood."

The old man leaned forward, the chair creaking under him.

"Those seventeen black beans, they weren't just a punishment. They were a reminder. A country's got to know when to stop chasin' the fight. Texas learned it the hard way. The lesson's still good."

He looked at the boy and gave a small, tired smile.

"That's the end of the Republic's wild years, son. After Mier, the flags got quieter, and the talk turned to joinin' the Union. Pride had cost us enough."

He stood, stretching his back, and nodded toward the dark horizon.

"Lessons in Humility"

The night had gone still again. The old man reached for the lantern wick and turned it down until the flame sat low and steady. The glow caught the lines in his face, deep as plow furrows.

"After Mier," he said, "the country settled into a kind of tired peace. Not the good kind. The kind that comes when you've run out of breath. Texas had proved she could fight, but she hadn't yet learned when to quit. Those seventeen men at the jar taught her that."

He rested both hands on his knees and looked out across the dark.

"We'd won our freedom at San Jacinto and nearly lost it to our own pride. The years that followed were quieter but heavier. Houston came back to office, patched what he could, and told folks to think less about glory and more about tomorrow. The talk turned from conquest to survival, from banners to fences. That's how a country grows up, when it finally learns the weight of its own mistakes."

The boy spoke softly. "Was that the end of the fightin'?"

The old man gave a slow shake of his head.

"Not hardly. Peace don't hold long in a land this wide. The border was still wild, the plains still dangerous, and the new Republic too broke to keep an army worth the name. So she called on the same kind of men who'd been ridin' since Austin's day, men who knew dust better than paper, who answered to no one but each other. The Rangers."

He shifted his weight and let the chair creak once before going on.

"They weren't soldiers, not really. They were scouts, lawmen, trackers, and sometime outlaws. But they held the line when there wasn't one. After Mier, it was their turn to take the saddle again. Texas had traded pride for duty, and those riders carried both."

He stood slowly, stretching his back, and took his hat from the post.

"You could say the Republic found its humility there on the Rio Grande, and she sent it ridin' north and west with the Rangers to guard what was left of her pride. That's the next piece of the story, the forts, the raids, the dust, and the men who tried to tame it."

He glanced back at the boy, eyes soft but steady.

"Get some rest," he said. "Tomorrow we'll ride with 'em. The nights were longer then, the land rougher, and the stories still smell of gunpowder and mesquite."

The lantern hissed as he turned the wick down, leaving the porch in darkness and the sound of wind moving through the trees, the same wind those riders once followed.

Chapter Eight

Riders for the Republic

"The Line Never Stopped Moving"

The wind had picked up again, whistling through the pecans and pushing a scatter of dust across the yard. The old man shifted his boots and held his hat in his lap like he was keeping it from blowing away.

"After Mier," he said, "the politicians went back to talkin' and the soldiers went home, but the war never really quit. It just moved out where the roads ended. You can call it peace if you like, but the frontier never heard the news."

He leaned forward, resting his elbows on his knees.

"Texas was her own country then, still flyin' the Lone Star, still broke, still fightin'. Houston was tryin' to build a nation out of paper, but out west and north, it was still about who could stay alive till morning. Every creek, every river bend, was a border no one agreed on. The Comanche, Kiowa, Wichita, and Lipan Apache still rode the plains like they always had. To them, the Republic was just another stranger plantin' fences in a country that never asked for 'em."

He rubbed his hands together, the sound dry in the air.

"Settlers kept comin' anyway. They built cabins along the Brazos, the Trinity, and the Colorado, draggin' their wagons into country that didn't want visitors. They'd plant a cornfield one spring and find it burned come fall. Folks in Austin called it expansion. The people livin' it called it survival, because for the poor and landless, they had no choices."

He took a slow breath.

"That's when the Rangers started ridin' regular again. They weren't new, Austin had used 'em before the Revolution, but now they were the only army the Republic could afford. No uniforms, no steady pay, just a promise of land if they lived long enough to claim it. **Jack Hays, Ben McCulloch, Henry Karnes, Mathew 'Old Paint' Caldwell**, and a few others gathered men who knew how to shoot straight and sleep light. The government in Austin called it protection. For the settlers it was just hope and a promise that better days were ahead."

He looked at the boy.

"Houston used to say the frontier was a line drawn in sand, and the wind kept movin' it. That was true enough. The Rangers were the only ones tryin' to hold that line. Some days they won, most days they just lasted."

He reached for the coffeepot, poured a swallow, and stared into it.

"The worst of it started in thirty-six, right after the war. The fight at Fort Parker was the first real bloodshed of the new Republic. A handful of families had built a little stockade up by the Navasota River, thinkin' thick logs could hold back a world. In May, a war party of Comanche, Kiowa, and a few Wichita hit at dawn. Killed most, took five captives, among 'em a girl named Cynthia Ann Parker, nine years old."

He paused, eyes gone far away.

"They carried her north into the plains. She grew up there, married a Comanche chief, and bore a son named Quanah. The Republic thought it had lost a child. What it really did was plant a seed. You'll hear more about him later. He'd be the one to remind Texas that the war between white and red never had just one side."

The boy shifted on the step. "Didn't the Rangers go after her?"

The old man nodded.

"They tried, but they were too few and too far behind. You can't chase shadows across that much prairie. After Fort Parker, Houston ordered patrols all the way from the Red River down to the Guadalupe. He said if Texas was gonna last, somebody had to ride watch over it. That's how the first Ranger companies of the Republic came to be, two dozen men in a company to guard a country bigger than a small kingdom."

He leaned back, the chair still creaking under his weight.

"They were young and half wild, sleepin' in their boots, ridin' with rifles across their laps. They fought raiders in the mesquite one day and hunted their own supper the next. They weren't heroes then, just men doin' what had to be done. The forts gave warnings, but it was the Rangers who gave people enough quiet to plant again."

The wind stirred the lantern flame. The old man looked toward the horizon, where the darkness met the land.

"Texas called herself free, but out here she was still fightin' for it every sunrise. The line between settled and savage never stopped movin'. It just changed who was standin' on which side."

He tipped his hat back and gave a small nod toward the boy.

"Now let's talk about the riders who followed that line, the ones who learned to live in the saddle and die without ceremony. They called 'em the Rangers, and they were the hardest answer Texas ever gave."

The Forts and the Riders

The old man took his hat off and set it on the rail, where the wind caught the brim and turned it once before settling.

"Now, the Republic was too broke for an army," he said. "So it built forts instead, small ones, scattered along the edge of settlement. Fort Houston near the Trinity, Fort Parker, where you already heard, Fort Griffin, Fort Milam, and a few more that never made it onto any map that lasted. They were built from logs cut close to the riverbanks, mud packed between the cracks, roofs that leaked when the first storm rolled through."

He scratched the side of his jaw.

"Those posts were never meant to win a war. They were there to warn the folks behind 'em that trouble was comin'. A bugle or a gunshot in the night, then fire on the horizon. By the time help rode out, the cabins were gone. But they kept buildin' anyway. A fort was a promise, even if it couldn't keep it."

He looked down and brushed a thin film of ash off his sleeve.

"The Rangers filled the gaps between those forts. "They went where the soldiers couldn't," he said. "Long rides, sometimes a week at a stretch, followin' the Brazos or the Llano or the Red. Most nights they slept on the ground with their saddles for pillows, the horses standin' close for warmth. Pay showed up when it could, which wasn't often. The only orders they ever understood were to watch, to fight if they had to, and to keep breathin'. Men like that didn't need much reason. Just somethin' that felt worth the dust."

He poured a swallow of coffee, then idly traced a circle around the rim of the cup with his finger.

"Jack Hays was the best of 'em, quiet, polite, but fast when he needed to be. He learned the Comanche trails like he'd been born to it, knew where the water lay hidden, and which canyons could hide a war party. He didn't chase every raid; he watched, waited, struck when the ground favored him. Folks said he could see through smoke. Maybe he could."

The boy asked, "Were they all like him?"

"Not hardly," the old man said, glancing at the boy with a wry smile. "Some were brave, some mean, some just lucky. A few were all three on the same day. Ben McCulloch, for instance, a steady shot, could fix a rifle with a hammer and a prayer. Henry Karnes rode till he dropped from fever, then got back up and rode again. Most of 'em didn't live long enough to grow old."

He flicked a moth away from the lantern glass.

"Their enemies were just as fierce. The Comanche called the Rangers 'wolf riders', part respect, part curse. The Kiowa and Wichita learned to listen for the echo of hooves before dawn. The Rangers gave as good as they got, sometimes worse. They weren't soldiers with rules; they were survivors with rifles."

He tipped his head toward the pasture.

"You already heard about Fort Parker, where the Parker family was wiped out, and that little girl was carried off. That raid set the tone for a decade. Every year after, there was another, cabins burned on the Colorado, families taken on the Llano, wagons cut off near San Antonio. The Rangers couldn't be everywhere, but they tried."

He shifted in his chair and rubbed his wrists.

"Thirty-nine and forty were the worst years. The Comanche had been pushed hard by sickness and hunger, and they came south in numbers nobody had seen before. The Council House Fight in San Antonio was supposed to make peace. The chiefs came in to talk, bringin' captives for trade. Somebody fired a shot inside the meeting hall, and by the time it was done, the floor was red. After that, peace wasn't even a word worth speakin'."

He stared into the lantern light.

"A few months later, a Comanche war party hit the settlements all the way down to Victoria and Linnville on the coast, near two hundred riders, burnin' and takin' whatever they pleased. The Rangers caught up with 'em near Lockhart, at a place that came to be called Plum Creek. That fight was chaos, gunsmoke, dust, and the cries of horses. The Comanche lost near eighty men that day. The Rangers called it a victory. The settlers called it revenge. I reckon it was both."

He pushed his coffee cup aside, its bottom scraping the wood.

"After Plum Creek, the frontier stayed bloody. Surveyin' parties vanished. But that had been goin; on for a few years. One group in thirty-eight was ambushed near where Dawson, Texas, stands now, a joint party of Kickapoo, Keechi Waco, and others. The Indians had warned the surveyors to leave, but pride took over and they ignored the warning. Soon they were jumped by a group of forty or so, but that number climbed quickly as more warriors joined the fight. Most of the party was killed, but a few got away, some with help from friendly Kickapoos. The ground there was scattered with the tools of their trade, chains, tripods, compasses, all busted up by the time their friends found 'em. A few Rangers and their friends buried what was left and rode on."

He stood, stretched, and stepped down off the porch a pace or two, boots crunching in the gravel.

"That's what the line looked like in those years, boy, a trail of burned cabins and fresh graves, held together by men who didn't know the word surrender. The forts were mileposts in a story written with smoke."

He turned back toward the house and leaned against the rail instead of sitting.

"Some nights I think about those riders, alone on the plains, hearin' the wind move through the grass and not knowin' if it was wind or riders comin'. They weren't lookin' for medals. They were lookin' for sunrise."

He let the wind carry his words a moment, then nodded toward the boy.

"Next part, we'll ride with 'em into the open country, where the fights never waited for orders and courage didn't ask permission. That's the story of the Rangers, and of the land that made 'em.

The Riders and the Reckoning

The old man leaned against the porch post instead of sitting, his shadow stretching long across the yard.

"By the time the fort line pushed north again," he said, "the Republic was nearly spent. Men like **Willie Boon** of Journey's Company would spend a few months in the saddle, and a few bringin' in crops for vittles for his wife. Ten years of fightin' had worn the Republic thin, too many raids, too many funerals, too many promises written on paper nobody could afford to keep. The Rangers were still ridin', but the country behind 'em had started talkin' about joinin' the Union. Texas was proud, but she was tired."

He turned his hat in his hands, thumb working the sweat-stained brim.

"When Houston came back into office, he said the best way to keep Texas safe was to make her part of somethin' bigger. Some called it betrayal; others, survival. The men ridin' the frontier didn't care much either way. The flag might change, but the wind and the dust stayed the same."

He looked up toward the stars, which were beginning to fade behind thin clouds.

"By forty-five, the deal was done. The Republic was gone, and Texas belonged to the United States. The Rangers swore new oaths, but they kept the same rifles and the same grudges. The line between law and wilderness still ran crooked through the heart of the country."

He stepped off the porch and walked a few paces toward the fence.

"After annexation, the raids didn't stop. If anythin', they got worse. Settlers kept comin', buildin' too fast, stretchin' the line thin again. The Rangers were still the only thing standin' between families and the wind. They knew the cost and paid it anyway."

He turned back toward the boy, voice low.

"Somewhere in all that ridin' came a name we already spoke, Cynthia Ann Parker. Twenty-four years after she was taken from Fort Parker, a Ranger patrol under Lawrence Sullivan Ross hit a Comanche camp on the Pease River. They didn't know who was there till the shootin' stopped. Among the captives was a woman with blue eyes and a Comanche husband lyin' dead beside her. She was cryin' for a baby killed in the fight."

The old man's jaw tightened.

"They brought her back to the settlements, said it was a rescue. Maybe it was, but she didn't see it that way. She'd been Comanche longer than she'd been Texan. She spoke no English, ate no white man's food, and never stopped mournin'. She died a few years later, heartsick. The Rangers said they'd done their duty. Maybe they had. But not every duty feels like a victory."

He took off his hat and brushed a bit of dust from the crown.

"Her son was still out there, Quanah, born of two worlds and belongin' to neither. He grew into a leader, the last chief of the Comanche. When his people finally came down from the plains, he walked at their head. Carried himself like his mother, proud, silent, with eyes that remembered everything. That was years after the Republic was gone, but he carried its ghost, just like the rest of us."

He sat again, slow and careful, the chair creaking beneath him.

"The frontier didn't end with a gunfight, boy. It ended when the land ran out of room for both sides to live free. The Rangers thought they'd tamed it, but all they really did was survive it. They held the line till there was no line left to hold."

The boy looked out into the dark, then back at him.

"Were they heroes?" he asked.

The old man thought on it for a long moment before answering.

"Some were. Some weren't. Most were just men ridin' for pay, pride, or penance. But they kept the country alive when it could've died, and that's worth rememberin'. You don't have to be pure to be important."

He tipped his head toward the horizon, where the first light of morning was pressing up against the stars.

"When you drive west someday, past the Pecos or up toward the Red, you'll still see the bones of those forts, half buried in grass. The wind hums through the old walls like it's still callin' roll. Listen close and you'll hear it, not the sound of war, but of men doin' their best with what they had."

He reached for the lantern, turned down the flame until it was nothing but a coal.

The old man looked off toward the north pasture, where the wind was starting to stir the grass.

"That was the end of the old line," he said. "The forts quieted down, and the riders hung up their guns for a spell. Texas later joined the Union, but it was still wild at the edges. The Rangers would ride again when the drums of war started up, and the land would bleed all over before it learned peace."

He reached down, dusted off his hat, and set it back on his head.

"After the war, there'd be a new kind of trail, not for soldiers, but for cattle. We were broke then, short on money and long on longhorns. The men who once fought to keep this country alive would saddle up again, drivin' herds north to feed a nation. That's another story, one of dust and distance."

He turned down the lantern flame until only the coal glowed red.

The next night came on slow, the air heavy with the smell of rain down south. The old man sat with the lantern low and his hat pulled forward, pipe smoke driftin' lazy in the light.

"That river we talked about," he said, "didn't just end a war. It started a job that never quit. The Rio Grande turned into a line that had to be guarded, and the Army came to do it. They built forts one after another, wood, stone, whatever they could haul, tryin' to hold back the wind, the raids, and the kind of men who didn't see borders. The Buffalo Soldiers rode there, Rangers too, watchin' the same horizon from different sides of the flag."

He leaned back, "That's where the real frontier began, not in victory or defeat, but in the work of keepin' peace one mile at a time. Every post, every patrol, every grave along that line wrote the next part of Texas."

The night came on heavy, air thick like it wanted to rain but didn't have the heart for it. The old man sat quietly for a while, pipe in hand, staring off before he spoke. "That fight with Mexico," he said, "it didn't just draw a line on a map. It showed Texas how small she really was."

He knocked the ash out of his pipe. "There weren't proper forts yet, none of the big stone posts folks talk about later. Just a few shacks of logs and dirt, and a handful of men wearin' beat-up hats and carryin' muskets older than they were. The Republic might've been gone on paper, but in most hearts it was still hangin' on, poor, proud, and half wild."

He raised his hat, scratched his head, then looked back toward the dark. "Those years, the Rangers were about all we had. They were the line between folks and the plains, between a cabin light and the wide unknown."

He thumbed the lantern wick down till the glow shrank to a coal. "Settle in, boy," he said. "We're still standin' in the Republic's shadow. The forts and soldiers will come later. For now, it's Rangers, settlers, and a country learnin' the hard way what freedom costs. When we joined the Union, we thought the fightin' was done for, we were plumb wrong."

Chapter Nine

The Mexican War: A Line in the Dust

Origins & the Disputed Ground (1836–1845)

The old man sat a while before he talked, as if the heat needed to settle. "The Mexican War didn't start in '46," he said. "It started the day we said the Rio Grande was ours, and Mexico said it wasn't."

He tipped the pipe bowl toward the yard. "Back in '36, after San Jacinto, the new Texas government made a treaty, The Treaty of **Velasco**, that set the **Rio Grande** as our border. Mexico never signed it proper. They said Santa Anna had no right to promise anything while tied up and thankin' his captors. As far as Mexico was concerned, the old line at the **Nueces** still held. So from the start, you had two rivers and one claim."

He drew a breath. "Between those rivers, Nueces to the north, Rio Grande to the south, was a strip of country that looked empty to a man who didn't know where to look. Thorn, mesquite, sand; long miles of heat and sky was everywhere. But ranches were there, and trails, and water if you'd been shown where to dig for it. Texans rode it and called it ours. Mexican patrols rode it and said the same. Every hoofprint was a dare."

He knocked ash from the pipe. "The Republic tried letters first. Sent men to **Mexico City** to talk recognition, sent others to **Washington** to talk annexation. Mexico answered with silence or soldiers; Washington answered with smiles and shrugs. The United States liked Texas well enough, but she didn't like the trouble that came with her. Slavery spooked the North. War with Mexico spooked the rest."

He worked his thumb along the rail. "Still, the idea of joining the Union never died out here. We were broke more years than not. Paper money worth less than the paper. Rangers are riding on promises. A country can have pride and still need help. By '45, the wind had shifted in Washington. **James K. Polk** took the oath with a map in his head, Atlantic to Pacific, and he meant to fit Texas into the hinge of it."

He looked over at the boy. "You ever hear grown men talk about destiny like it pays their bills? That was the talk back then, **Manifest Destiny**. Pretty words for a land hunger that could chew through mountains. Polk didn't hide it much. He sent feelers for **California** and New

Mexico; let it be known the Union wanted harbors on the far water and a road to reach 'em."

He set the pipe down and laced his fingers. "Mexico saw it clear enough. Recognize Texas, lose pride. Refuse, risk war. They chose refusal and hoped the United States would blink. Polk didn't. He sent **General Zachary Taylor** to the southern edge of Texas with orders to protect us. Taylor marched into the disputed strip and built a fort near **Matamoros**. Mexico called that invasion. Texas disagreed and called it protection. Truth was, it was both, depending on which river a man saluted."

He paused, then added, "Through those Republic years, Rangers kept the line from comin' apart. Not a straight line, not on any map, just the space where cabins could stand a season without burnin'. **Penateka Comanche** still ranged the hill country; **Karankawa** survivors still haunted the bays; Mexican cavalry still patrolled the lower brush. The **Council House Fight** had poisoned half the peace talks up north. Down south, the **Rio Grande** was a long whisper, traders, smugglers, families, all moving as they always had while governments argued over names."

He gave the boy a sidelong glance. "People think borders are drawn in ink. Mostly, they're drawn in footsteps and fear. A widow whose boys herd south of the Nueces doesn't care which Congress said what; she cares which set of uniforms shows up first. Same went for ranchers along the lower river. They branded on one side and married on the other."

He shifted his hat. "By late '45, the annexation papers were signed. Texas was in. Mexico broke relations with the United States and called us thieves with friends in high places. Washington sent Taylor deeper into the disputed strip with the kind of orders that don't look like orders when the newspapers print 'em. Taylor wasn't flashy. He just did what soldiers do, built, drilled, waited."

He rubbed at a scar near his wrist. "All the while, that strip of land, the **Nueces Strip**, folks call it now, was grinding the edge off patience. A Mexican patrol rides up to check a crossing; Texans say invasion. A Texan scouting party pushes down to a water hole; Mexico says provocation. If a storm lasted that long over the Gulf, every man would know a hurricane was comin'. This was a storm made of paper, pride, and men who didn't back their horses away from an argument."

He leaned forward, voice low. "So understand this: the war started because two governments claimed the same ground and both thought the other would blink. Texas wasn't just a prize. She was the doorway. Through it lay **New Mexico, California**, and a dream big enough for politicians to stand on and call it holy."

He sat back. "There were other strings tied on this bundle, slavery among 'em. Every new acre would ask the same hard question, free or slave, and the country would answer different depending on which state counted the votes. That's not Mexico's war; that's ours. But the road to that question ran straight through this one."

He let out a breath. "By spring **1846**, Taylor's men were counting days and shoveling dirt. Mexican cavalry was counting the same days on the other bank. A patrol met a column in the thorn. Shots fired. Dead on both sides. Polk told Congress what Congress was waiting to hear: American blood, American soil. They voted for war faster than an undertaker can measure a pine box."

He nodded toward the south as if he could see the river from the porch. "That's the start. Not glory. Not songs. A strip of brush called by two different names and a lot of men who didn't know yet what they were riding into."

He lifted the pipe again but didn't light it. "Write it down in your book the way it deserves, boy: **Treaty of Velasco** said Rio Grande; **Mexico** said Nueces; the land between was a fuse. **Annexation** put a match to it. **Polk** blew on the flame. The wind did the rest."

He stood, stretched his back till it popped, then settled again. "Now we can talk about how the thing played out, Taylor's steady hand, Scott's long march, and the Texans who rode ahead of both of 'em. But first you had to know why the ground itself was angry."

Annexation & the Road to War (1845–Spring 1846)

The old man struck a match, lit the pipe, and puffed till the glow came steady. "When Texas signed up with the Union," he said, "it was a wedding half the country didn't want to attend. Mexico called it theft. The anti-slavery Northern papers called it trouble. Down here, we called it survival, we just simply had no choice. We were flat out of options."

He leaned back, eyes half shut. "You can't blame Texans for sayin' yes. The Republic was broke, her army worn thin, and her money was worth more for wallpaper than trade. The dream was still good, but dreams don't feed families. Annexation meant safety, trade, and a treasury that didn't bounce. It also meant borrowin' Washington's enemies."

He twisted his head to take a crick out of his neck before proceeding, "Mexico took it like a slap. They'd warned the States that annexin' Texas would mean war, but Washington had ears only for the sound of opportunity. Polk wanted California and New Mexico; Texas was just the key that opened that door. The Rio Grande claim gave him a reason to unlock it."

He drew on his pipe, the ember glowing. "Early '46, Polk sent **General Zachary Taylor** south to guard Texas. Taylor was a soldier's soldier, plain, quiet, steady. No fancy drill or speeches, do your work and eat when you can. His orders said to hold the line, but nobody could agree on which line that was. He built **Fort Texas** near the Rio

Grande, right across from the Mexican town of **Matamoros**. Mexico called it an invasion. Taylor thought it was caution. Neither side was wrong, and that's what made it dangerous."

The boy tilted his head. "Didn't anybody try to stop it?"

The old man smiled. "A few. **Sam Houston**, sittin' in Austin, told folks the blood of Texas had already filled one river, and he wasn't keen on fillin' another. But he wasn't in charge no more, and Washington's men weren't listenin'. The Congress up north argued for about a week, then voted for a war most of 'em thought would be over by Christmas."

He took the pipe out of his mouth and gestured with it. "Taylor's army was a strange outfit, regular soldiers, militia from Louisiana and Mississippi, and a few hundred Texas volunteers who weren't used to takin' orders. Some wore uniforms, some wore buckskins, and a good many wore out their shoes before they ever crossed the river. The Rangers joined in, ridin' ahead of Taylor's column, scoutin' trails, lookin' for water, and stirrin' up as much trouble as they found."

He chuckled low. "Those Rangers were a breed apart, **Jack Hays**, **Ben McCulloch**, **Samuel Walker**, men who could find a trail in a thunderstorm and still be laughin' at dawn. The regular army didn't know what to do with 'em. Polk liked the results, though. When you're fightin' a country that big, you need men who don't mind goin' off the map."

He knocked the ashes from the bowl, eyes on the yard. "On April 25, 1846, a patrol under Captain Thornton rode into the scrub near the Rio Grande and ran headlong into a column of Mexican lancers. They fought a short fight, outnumbered, surrounded, half killed or captured. It was small, as battles go, but the headlines made it thunder. Polk told Congress, 'American blood on American soil,' and that was all he needed. Two days later, the vote was done. War."

He pointed south. "That's how easy it starts, boy. One river, two governments, and a patrol that didn't know which way the wind was blowin'. Polk got the war he wanted, Mexico got the fight she couldn't afford, and Texas got pulled into somethin' bigger than any of us expected."

The boy looked down at his notes. "Wasn't there any way to stop it?"

"Maybe," the old man said. "But you can't stop a country that believes it's actin' on destiny. Men with that kind of faith will march through a hurricane if the map says paradise is on the other side."

He shifted his weight, the chair creaking. "So the armies gathered. Polk called for fifty thousand volunteers. Most of 'em came from the South, Georgia, Tennessee, Mississippi, Texas. Northerners weren't keen on dyin' for what they figured was slaveholders' land. But Polk didn't care where the men came from as long as they showed up."

He took another puff. "Taylor's troops crossed the river that spring. The Mexican soldiers waited for 'em on the flat scrub near **Palo Alto**: hot day, open ground, artillery on both sides. The Americans fired slow and steady, new light guns that shot farther and faster than anything Mexico had. By sundown, the Mexicans pulled back. Two days later, at **Resaca de la Palma**, they hit again, close fightin' this time. The Rangers led the charge, ridin' through musket fire like a stampede. When it ended, the Mexican army was across the river, leavin' behind cannon, wounded, and pride."

He nodded slowly. "Those two fights set the tone for the whole war. Quick, mean, and costly. Taylor crossed the river, took **Matamoros**, then pushed deeper into Mexico. By summer, his men were on the march to **Monterrey**, draggin' wagons through heat thick enough to melt tin."

He looked at the boy. "That's where we'll pick it up next, the march south, the names that mattered, and the Texans who rode ahead of the army and gave it eyes. The fightin' didn't make heroes right away, but it made soldiers out of men who'd never seen a map bigger than their own county."

The boy nodded, pencil scratchin' the page. "What should I call this part?"

The old man smiled. "Call it what it was, the road to war. Every step down it was paved with pride, politics, and a river full of misunderstandin's.

The Fighting & the Texans (1846–1847)

The old man lit his pipe again, puffed a few times, and watched the smoke rise. "Once Taylor crossed the Rio Grande," he said, "the war stopped bein' a question of borders and started bein' a question of pride. And when pride gets involved, wars last longer than anybody plans."

He shifted his hat. "Taylor marched south toward **Monterrey**, the city of the mountains. It was September of '46, hot as the devil's kitchen, and the air smelled like dust and soldiers sweat. The Mexican general there, **Pedro de Ampudia**, had near ten thousand men. Taylor had maybe six. But he also had men who knew how to fight without orders."

He smiled, "That's where the Texans came in. The **Rangers** and volunteers rode ahead of the army, scoutin' passes, watchin' water holes, bringin' back word of the Mexican lines. They fought house to house when the army hit Monterrey, Rangers on rooftops, muskets flashin', lancers comin' down side streets. **Ben McCulloch** and **Jack Hays** led men through courtyards while cannon smoke rolled through the alleys. When it was over, the city was taken and both sides were too tired to call it victory."

He tapped the pipe against the rail. "That battle showed the generals somethin'. Regular soldiers fight by orders;

Rangers fight by instinct. Taylor didn't always like it, but he learned to use it. He said the Rangers were rough as rawhide, but worth their weight in lead. The Mexicans called 'em devils, and they were closer to the truth."

The boy looked up. "Didn't McCulloch work with Taylor again?"

"More than once," the old man said. "McCulloch scouted the whole north country for him. Rode ahead of the columns, mapped passes, found the enemy, slipped back with news. Carried dispatches through fire at **Buena Vista** later on, and without him, a few thousand men might've gone missin'."

He turned the pipe stem between his fingers. "After Monterrey, Taylor moved deeper in. Santa Anna himself came back from exile to stop him, marchin' north with near fifteen thousand men. Taylor had five. They met in February '47 at a place called **Buena Vista**, a wide plateau cut with ravines. It was cold, windy, and full of dust. The Mexican army rolled in with drums and banners; Taylor's boys waited behind low walls and wagons. For two days, the fight swung like a gate in the wind. Cannon spoke, cavalry charged, smoke rolled. The Rangers were there, coverin' flanks, cuttin' off attacks, ridin' hard through the dust."

He paused, eyes half-closed as if he could see it. "**Albert Sidney Johnston** was there, servin' as inspector under Taylor. He kept order when the volunteers started runnin'.

Calm man, steady. You'll hear his name again when the country splits. Some said he was the only officer Taylor trusted to do the job right."

The boy scribbled the name down. "What about the others?"

The old man smiled faintly. "**Edward Burleson** led Texans in the northern campaigns, an old Revolution hand who couldn't stay home. **Mirabeau B. Lamar** rode as a lieutenant colonel, fightin' more with his pride than his sword. He said politics were dead to him, but politics never die easy. He rode well, though. Men followed him because he looked like a man who believed what he said."

He puffed his pipe. "After **Buena Vista**, the fightin' shifted south. General **Winfield Scott** landed an army at **Veracruz**, biggest landin' this country had ever seen, cannons on the beach, ships shellin' the city, white sand turnin' black with powder smoke. Once the walls fell, Scott started marchin' toward **Mexico City**. The Rangers scouted for him again, Hays, McCulloch, and men from every Texas settlement that still had a horse to spare. They moved ahead of the army, ridin' through cactus and stone, bringin' back word of roads and ambushes."

The old man's voice dropped low. "That road chewed men up," he said. "One hill after another, one town after the next. **Cerro Gordo, Contreras, Churubusco, Molino del Rey, Chapultepec,** each name a grave if you ask the ones who were there. The air was thick with it, powder smoke, sweat, sickness, all mixed together. The ground stayed muddy, never had time to dry, soaked with rain and blood both. The Mexican boys fought hard, no denyin' that. They still had pride, and they showed it. Brave men, tough as rawhide, but hungry and near out of powder, still tryin' to follow orders from a government that was already fallin' apart..A man can only hold his ground so long on an empty stomach and a promise that don't feed him. By September, Scott's army was walkin' through the streets of Mexico City, the fight gone but the hurt still hangin' in the air. The fight was done, though the dyin' kept at it awhile longer." The war was over, though no one was ready to admit it yet."

He set the pipe down and looked at the boy. "You know what's funny? The same officers who fought together there would turn their guns on each other fifteen years later. **Robert E. Lee**, **Ulysses Grant**, **Longstreet**, **Meade**, **Jefferson Davis**, and **Albert Sidney Johnston**, all wore the same uniform in Mexico. They learned the trade of war together, side by side, and they'd use every lesson again when the country came apart. That's why they call it the schoolhouse of the generals."

The boy nodded slowly, pencil scratching. "So, Texas helped teach 'em?"

"Helped teach the world," the old man said. "The Rangers showed 'em what cavalry could do when it wasn't tied to drill books. The Texans showed the army that men who live by the saddle fight different. That mix of regular and rough made a new kind of soldier, one who could read country like a map and use it like a weapon. You'll see it again when **Hood's Texans** march east."

He leaned back, eyes on the horizon. "War makes soldiers. Sometimes it makes monsters. Mexico saw both. The Rangers earned fear and respect in the same breath. Some fought fair; some didn't. There's tales of raids that went too far, villages hit harder than they should've been. War don't care about saints, and no army has ever kept its halo clean."

He rubbed the bridge of his nose. "By the time the smoke cleared, Taylor was a national hero, Scott was a candidate for president, and most Texans were headin' home broke but proud. They'd ridden under a flag that wasn't theirs, but they'd proven their worth to the nation that adopted 'em. Texas had become the edge of a country that thought itself unstoppable."

He looked at the boy again. "And that's where the next trouble started. The war gave us a border, sure enough, but it gave us somethin' else, a habit of pushin' west till the ocean stopped us. The United States had its reach, but now it had to figure out what to do with its arms full."

He smiled without humor. "That'll take us to the treaty and what came after, the Rio Grande fixed on a map and Texas suddenly holdin' the front door of an empire.

But borders don't stay put, and rivers don't quit runnin'. You'll see."

The Treaty and the Border That Wouldn't Sleep

The old man knocked his pipe clean, filled it again, and didn't bother to light it. "Every war ends on paper first," he said. "Took 'em two years of killin' to start talkin' peace, and two weeks of talkin' to argue about who owned the dust."

He leaned forward, forearms on his knees. "They met at a little church outside Mexico City, **Guadalupe Hidalgo**. The ink dried in February of '48. Mexico gave up nearly half of her country, **California, New Mexico, Arizona, Nevada, Utah**, and pieces of **Colorado and Wyoming**. The United States paid $15 million and promised to keep the line at the **Rio Grande**. It looked neat on the map, but the land itself didn't much notice."

He looked toward the south. "That treaty made winners out of Washington and losers out of folks who never fought. Ranchers woke up in Mexico one morning and went to bed in the United States that night without movin' a fencepost. Families split down the middle, half their kin on the far bank, half on this one. Merchants called it opportunity; everyone else it was confusion."

He rubbed the bowl of his pipe. "For Texas it was a strange sort of victory," he said. "We finally got the border we'd been claimin' since Velasco, but we also got stuck watchin' it. The **Rio Grande** wasn't any wall, it was a road, and it ran both ways. Traders, smugglers, runaways, all usin' the same crossings. Every time the river flooded it slid a little, changed its bed, and every change started the argument all over again."

He gave a dry laugh. "The soldiers that stayed behind tried to hold the peace the only way they knew," he said. "They built forts, **Brown**, **Inge**, **Clark**, **Duncan**, not much more than logs, rock, and hope set down along the river. They called it a frontier line, but it was really just a handful of lonely posts strung out through bad country. The Rangers rode the empty ground between 'em, coverin' more miles than made sense, keepin' watch on a border that never sat still." The Mexicans had their rurales on the other side doin' the same thing. Two uniforms, one kind of dust."

The boy asked, "Was it peace?"

The old man shook his head. "Peace on paper, maybe. The kind you sign with one hand and draw your pistol with the other. Raids still came, cattle went missin', smugglers ran whiskey and slaves both. Every treaty brings a new kind of trouble. This one was no different."

He stretched his legs. "The river kept its own time. Some years it ran wide, others it shrank to a trickle. When it moved, so did the line, and each side swore the other had stolen ground. Lawyers called it arbitration; the Rangers called it another reason to ride. The Rio Grande never sleeps, boy. Still doesn't."

He looked off toward the dark horizon. "That war gave the United States her ocean dream, but it gave Texas a full-time headache. We were the edge of everything now, the border, the trade, the fights that never got big enough to make the papers but still filled the cemeteries."

He tapped the rail once for emphasis. "And all the while, the men who'd fought down in Mexico were comin' home. Some wore new medals, some just new scars. They'd seen cities bigger than they'd imagined, armies larger than the whole Republic had ever fielded. They brought back stories, pride, and the taste of somethin' that felt like destiny. That taste would sour soon enough."

He turned toward the boy. "Before long, the same officers who'd marched together under Scott and Taylor would be pickin' sides in another war, this one closer to home. But that's for later. For now, remember this, **Guadalupe Hidalgo** fixed a line and changed a nation, but it didn't fix the land. The border's been hummin' ever since, and we've been listenin' to it."

Training Ground for the Next War (1847–1850s)

The old man leaned back, pipe resting cold in his hand. "The war ended, but the army didn't pack up and go home," he said. "It just moved north and west. The veterans stayed, and most of the young officers kept their commissions. Texas turned into their classroom, same as Mexico had been their test."

He glanced at the boy. "You'd be surprised who rode our dirt in those years. The names that would fill history books later were all here first, **Albert Sidney Johnston**, **Robert E. Lee**, **George Thomas**, **E. Kirby Smith**, **John Bell Hood**, and a handful of others who'd end up fightin' each other before long. They learned the trade of war right here, ridin' between forts that barely had roofs."

He rubbed the rail with his thumb. "After the Mexican War, the United States was bigger, but it wasn't settled. The Comanche still owned most of the high country. The Army needed a regiment built for that kind of work, fast, hard, and mean enough to ride for days. So in **1855**, they formed the **Second U.S. Cavalry**, and they sent it to Texas."

He smiled faintly. "That outfit was somethin'. "Albert Sidney Johnston was the colonel," he said, "Texan by choice and also by spirit. His right hand was **Robert E. Lee**. Workin' under 'em were men you'll hear about later, **George Thomas**, **William Hardee**, **Van Dorn**, and a young fella named **John Bell Hood**. They trained out here in the heat, **Fort Mason**, **Fort Phantom Hill**, **Camp Cooper**, **Fort Chadbourne**, and a handful of lonely posts you'd have to squint to spot on a map today. The sun did most of the teachin'. It baked the polish off 'em and left nothin' but discipline and grit.". That regiment was the sharpest blade the army ever drew before the big split."

The boy looked up. "Did they fight the Indians?"

"They did, sure enough," the old man said. "The **Comanche** still had the high country. Knew every trail and trick of it. Draws, water holes, short cuts, places no soldier could find twice."

He spat into the dust. "Those cavalry boys had to learn it the hard way. Dust in their mouths till they were chewin' grit. Sun beat the hide right off their necks. Every now and then, an arrow'd whisper past, close enough to feel the air move. Made a man flinch before he knew why."

He paused, jaw tight. "Horses gave out before noon. When one dropped, you slung the saddle and kept walkin'. Grass came up to the stirrups, thick as brush. They slept on their coats with rifles across their knees. Woke to hoofbeats they couldn't tell were wind, buffalo, or trouble. That's how they learned the plains, slow, sore, half scared, followin' trails the Comanche drew with hooves instead of maps."

"They chased raiders from the **Llano Estacado** clear down to the **Rio Grande**, learnin' the only way a man can out there, ride light, strike fast, and pray the horse lasts another mile. The tricks they picked up huntin' Comanche would come back on 'em later. Same dust, same wind, only different uniforms."

He took a slow breath. "That was the last good peace the country had, if you can call it peace. The forts were thin, the pay late, but the army was young and proud. Lee wrote home about the sunsets over the Brazos, said it was beautiful and lonesome. Johnston kept the regiment together, quiet and strict. Thomas was fair but firm. Hood was reckless even then, full of fire, always wantin' to be where the bullets would be thickest."

He smiled, then frowned again. "They were soldiers before they were enemies. When the storm of secession came, that regiment split like dry wood. Lee went east to Virginia. Johnston took the call from the South. Thomas stayed with the Union. Hood followed Johnston into gray. Every man carried what he'd learned in Texas, the feel of the saddle, the sound of the wind before trouble. The Civil War was born out of those camps as much as it was out of politics."

He knocked the ash from his pipe. "That's what the Mexican War gave us, a bigger country and a generation of fighters. They'd seen what ambition looked like in uniform. They'd seen how fast courage could turn into habit. And they'd learned that wars don't end when you sign a treaty; they wait for new flags."

He looked down at the boy. "Texas was their forge, boy. The heat that shaped the blades. They came here young, ridin' the frontier. They left older and sharper, carryin' the dust of this land into the biggest fight this country ever had."

He stood, stretched his back till it popped, and looked out toward the southern sky where the stars were gatherin'. "That's the next story, the one where the country splits in two and Texas has to pick her side. It's called the Civil War, but around here we call it the time when brothers stopped speakin' and started shootin'."

He tipped his hat toward the boy. "We'll take that one tomorrow night. It's a long story, and it deserves a fresh pot of coffee."

Chapter Ten

The War That Changed Texas

The War Came Quiet

The old man turned the pipe in his hands, the bowl cool against his palm. The lantern beside him was near burned out, throwing more shadow than light across the boards.

"The war didn't start with music or marches," he said after a bit. "Out here it came quiet, letters, talk, folks arguin' about rights and pride. Nobody said much about the graves waitin' down the road."

He shifted in his chair and looked toward the boy.

"Texas went with the South for reasons as tangled as mesquite roots. Most folks who came here had come up from places like Alabama, Georgia, and the Carolinas. They'd brought their ways with 'em, their songs, their manners, and their belief that the world ran on cotton and people to pick it. Slavery wasn't just a practice; it was property, the same as a barn or a herd. It was the one thing the planters swore no man could take from them."

He rubbed the bowl of the pipe with his thumb, the sound dry against the wood.

"By eighteen sixty-one, the talk of secession had been blowin' around for years. Some said the North was gettin' too bossy, others said Washington was forgettin' who fed the nation. But deep down, everyone knew what it was really about, the right to keep another human bein' as work stock. The rich wanted to keep it, and the poor were told it was their duty to defend it. That's how a lie gets legs."

The chair creaked as he leaned forward.

"When the vote came, Texas followed her kin. The men in Austin declared the Union broken, said we'd stand with the Confederacy. Folks cheered in the towns, bands played, and preachers called it God's will. Only one man stood in the way, **Sam Houston**, governor then, old but still carryin' the weight of San Jacinto on his shoulders. He begged 'em to stay in the Union. Said war would bleed us dry. He told the Legislature, 'Mark my words, if Texas goes to war, it'll be ruin, defeat, and thousands of dead sons.'"

He looked toward the yard, where the trees moved just a little in the night breeze.

"They didn't listen. Pride don't have ears. When they made him swear loyalty to the Confederacy, he refused.

They turned him out of office like a man too worn for his own porch. He went home to Huntsville and stayed there while the storm he'd warned about rolled in."

He lifted the pipe to his lips but didn't light it.

"East Texas went gray first, planters sendin' their sons to join the southern regiments. The frontier counties and the hill country weren't so sure. The German settlers out near Fredericksburg and New Braunfels leaned toward the Union, saying they'd already left one king and didn't need another. Some refused to fight, and for that they paid with their lives."

He shook his head.

"Out here, it wasn't politics anymore. It was neighbors. Friends stopped speakin'. Churches split their prayers in two. Some folks stitched gray uniforms; others hid their loyalty under their breath. You could tell what side a man was on by which way he looked when the flag passed."

He tapped the pipe against the porch rail and watched a bit of ash fall through the cracks.

"The war didn't hit Texas all at once. It crept in slow, like bad weather on the horizon. First came the drills, the marches, the letters home sayin' it'd be over by Christmas. Then the news of battles, **Manassas**, **Antietam**, **Gettysburg**, names that meant nothin' till they came back written on telegrams. The graves started fillin' before folks even knew where those places were."

He took a slow breath.

"When the war finally reached Texas, it came like a storm that didn't know when to quit. It left the land poorer, the people divided, and the sky heavy with smoke that took years to clear."

He looked at the boy, his eyes steady.

"Freedom's a fine thing, but we keep learnin' the hard way it don't come free. Not for a country. Not for anybody."

Texans in Gray and Blue

The old man thumbed a fleck of tobacco off his knee.

"When the war got goin', it didn't come ridin' over the hills right away," he said. "It pulled men east instead, fathers, sons, brothers, marchin' toward a fight most of 'em couldn't even point to on a map. They said it was for states' rights, for honor, for Texas. But mostly it was for habit. Folks fight for the places they know."

He tilted the pipe bowl and tapped it lightly against his boot heel.

"More than seventy thousand Texans wore gray before it was over. Some joined for pay that never came, others because their neighbors did. A few went the other way, stayed loyal to the Union, or didn't believe in the cause to start with. There were Texans in blue uniforms too, though they were careful who they told about it."

He leaned forward, the chair sighing beneath his weight.

"The best-known of the lot was **Hood's Texas Brigade**, the pride of the Confederacy, they called it. They fought in Virginia under **General John Bell Hood**, a man who led from the front and lost near everything doin' it. His boys marched farther and bled harder than most. Gaines' Mill, Sharpsburg, Gettysburg, names that still ring like hammer blows. They charged till their flags were holes and their boots had more mud than leather."

He took a drink of coffee that had gone cold, wincing a little at the taste.

"They wrote home about glory. The families wrote back about crops gone bad and children who didn't understand where their daddies had gone. By sixty-three, most of those letters were comin' from hospitals instead of camps."

The wind moved through the trees, rustlin' the leaves like whispers.

"There were horsemen too," he went on. "**Terry's Texas Rangers**, they called themselves, the Eighth Texas Cavalry. Rode with Forrest and Bragg, fought from Kentucky to Georgia. They never lost a banner and seldom a fight. But it cost 'em. Half the regiment was dead or crippled by the end."

He set the empty cup down and rubbed his hands together slowly.

"Not all the war was fought somewhere else. It touched our own coast. In sixty-two, Union ships took **Galveston**, thinkin' to hold the port. Come New Year's Day of sixty-three, **General John B. Magruder** took it back. He lined steamboats with cotton bales for armor and floated right into the harbor, firin' cannon till the water boiled. It worked. The Yankees pulled out, and Galveston stayed Confederate till the end."

He smiled faintly, though his eyes didn't.

"Up the coast at **Sabine Pass**, forty-seven Irish volunteers under **Dick Dowling** held off a whole fleet. Two cannon, a little luck, and a lot of stubborn. They sank two Union gunboats and sent the rest runnin'. Folks called it a miracle; Dowling's men just called it good shootin'."

The boy shifted, half awed, half puzzled. "Sounds like Texas never lost."

The old man's smile faded.

"On paper, maybe. In truth, every victory came home as a letter edged in black. The state gave its sons to battles far from here, and they came back one by one, limpin' or not at all. Hood's Brigade went to war with more than two thousand men and came back with less than three hundred still standin'. The war took the best of a generation and left their families starin' at empty fields."

He looked out toward the pasture. The grass moved in slow waves under the wind.

"Most of Texas never heard the cannon, but we felt the echo. Prices went high, salt ran short, and every town lost someone. The pride that sent men marchin' east turned to sorrow by the time they reached home, if they did at all."

He stood for a moment, stretching the stiffness from his legs, and leaned one hand on the porch rail.

"That's what war does, boy. It takes what you've got and sends it wanderin'. The folks who stayed behind learned to make do with less and pray for the day the shootin' stopped."

He turned back toward the lantern's dim glow.

"Next part of it ain't about the fightin' men. It's about the ones left behind, the women, the old, and the young. They fought their own kind of war right here at home."

The Home Front and the Frontier

The old man rubbed his thumb along the edge of the coffee cup, eyes on the glow of the lantern.

"While the fight was goin' on back east," he said, "Texas was fightin' her own kind of war right here at home. The soldiers were gone, and what they left behind was worry, dust, and women tryin' to hold the roof over their heads."

He took a slow breath.

"With the men gone, the frontier slipped backward. The forts went quiet, and the **Comanche** and **Kiowa** came ridin' down again. Raids that used to stop at the Llano pushed clear toward the Colorado. Folks in the hill country packed what they could and headed east, leavin' cabins half built and fields half plowed. Houston used to say the frontier was a line drawn in the sand. During the war, that line washed away."

He set the cup down with a soft clink.

"The women did what they could. They plowed the fields with mules too old for the job and boys too young to push a plow. They boiled mesquite beans for coffee, spun thread from what cloth they could find, and patched shirts till they were more patch than cloth. My grandmother used to tell me how she'd save bacon grease to make candles and soap, and how she learned to make lye from ashes. She said war made every house a small army."

The boy leaned forward. "Was there ever any help?"

The old man shook his head.

"Not much. The state was broke, and the Confederacy had bigger fires to put out. What little the government sent west was gone before it got past Austin. A few old Rangers tried to hold the line, but it was like patchin' a roof in a rainstorm, you could never get ahead of the leaks."

He pushed his hat back on his head.

"The worst of it wasn't the raids, though. It was fear. You could smell it on the wind. Folks stopped trustin' each other. In the north, up around **Gainesville**, that fear turned mean. Some men there said the war was wrong, that Texas ought to stay with the Union. The rest called 'em traitors. In sixty-two, they rounded up near two hundred of 'em and built a gallows in the town square. Called themselves a 'Citizens Court.' Forty-one men were hanged before it was done."

He rubbed the bridge of his nose, as if the thought itself hurt.

"Some of the ones they killed had done nothin' but speak their minds. The war gave people excuses for things they'd never have stomached in peacetime. They said it was about loyalty. It was really about fear. When a country splits in two, the crack runs through every family."

He turned the cup in his hands again, then looked out across the pasture where the trees swayed in the dark.

"The farther west you went, the harder it got. Raidin' parties hit places like **Blanco**, **Burnet**, and **San Saba**. Small towns like **Mason** and **Menardville** emptied out overnight. Families headed east toward Brenham and Nacogdoches, hopin' the army would come back before the next moon. It never did."

He stood and stretched, the joints in his knees popping softly.

"Out on the coast, things were just as bad in a different way. Union ships kept the ports under blockade. Salt ran out first. Folks dug pits near the bays and boiled seawater by the barrel. The air smelled like brine and smoke. No coffee, no sugar, no steel. The women traded eggs for thread, and the men melted down old horseshoes to make nails."

He brushed a moth from the lantern glass and watched it spiral into the night.

"You hear people talk about heroes and battles, but this part, this was the real test. The folks who stayed behind were fightin' a war without guns. They fought hunger, loneliness, and the dark. When the war finally ended, they were the ones who still had to stand on both feet and start over."

He looked back at the boy, the lines in his face deep under the low light.

"The soldiers came home to nothin' but fences fallin' and crops gone to seed. Half of 'em came back different, some missin' limbs, some just quiet. The ones who didn't come back left holes in the world that never did close. You can still feel it in some towns, that hush when somebody says the word 'war.'"

He leaned both hands on the porch rail.

"That's what Texas learned, boy, that wars don't end when the shootin' stops. They keep echoing through the houses and the hearts of whoever's left."

He gave a small nod.

"Next came the hardest lesson, losin' without knowin' it yet. The fight was over back east, but it would be months before Texas heard the truth. And when the word came, it carried freedom and sorrow in the same breath."

The End of the War and Juneteenth

The old man watched the lantern's flame dance in the wind. "By sixty-five," he said, "the war was all but over everywhere else. Texas just hadn't heard it yet. The telegraph wires were down, the roads were washed out, and the men still under arms didn't know who'd won or lost."

He set the cup aside and rubbed the back of his neck.

"The last fight came in **May of eighteen sixty-five**, down near **Brownsville**, at a place called **Palmito Ranch**. It was fought a month after **Lee** had surrendered in Virginia. Nobody told the soldiers here. They went at it like the war still mattered, blue coats and gray ones clashin' in the heat. The Confederates won that little scrap, but it didn't mean a thing. You can win the last fight and still lose the war."

He sighed. "The surrender came slowly. By June, the Union army had reached **Galveston**. On the **nineteenth**, a general named **Gordon Granger** stood on the docks and read **General Order Number Three**, saying the war was done, the Union whole again, and every enslaved person free from that day forward. The crowd didn't know whether to cheer or cry. Some did both."

He looked toward the boy. "Word spread the way it always does in Texas, slow but sure. From Galveston to Houston, from Houston to the Brazos, from the Brazos clear up to the Red. Folks said it felt like rain after a long drought, but rain don't fix a field overnight. Freedom came with empty pockets and a thousand hard choices. Some stayed where they were, workin' the same land for wages that didn't stretch. Others took to the roads, lookin' for kin they hadn't seen in years. The world had turned over, but it wasn't steady yet."

He stood and stepped to the edge of the porch, staring out into the dark.

"The soldiers came home after that, those who still could. The gray coats were faded, the rifles rusted, and the faces older than their years. They found what was left, fences fallen, fields bare, barns burned. The women who'd kept the homes were tired down to the bone. But they made do. They always had."

He turned the brim of his hat between his fingers.

"Texas was broke, beat, and half in ashes. But pride don't die easy here. Folks couldn't accept that the war had been for nothin', so they made somethin' out of it. Called it The Lost Cause. Said the South had fought for honor, not for slaves. They told it enough times that they started believin' it. The stories grew taller with each retellin', generals made noble, defeats turned to near victories. It was a way to bury shame under stone and carve it into memory."

He let out a long breath.

"You can't blame 'em, not all the way. They'd given too much not to believe it meant somethin'. But it kept us blind longer than it should've. The war was over, but the fight to understand it was just beginnin'."

The Long Walk Home

The night had gone quiet again. The old man sat back down and pulled the lantern closer, the flame barely holding.

"When the guns quit talkin', the reckonin' began," he said. "We had to rebuild from dust, and every nail we drove carried the sound of the past. The South called it losin'; the preachers called it testin'; the widows called it silence. But life went on. Always does."

He looked at the boy, eyes soft beneath the shadow of his hat.

"Out of that ruin came the Texas we still talk about, rough, broke, but alive. The war taught us what pride costs, and the years after taught us how to work again. The old flags got folded away, but the memories didn't. Folks kept tellin' stories about honor and valor because the truth was too heavy to lift."

He leaned forward, elbows on his thighs.

"After a while, they started findin' another kind of fight, one they could win. Cattle were everywhere, runnin' wild across the prairie. There wasn't much else left worth sellin'. So, the men who'd once ridden for the South took to the trails, drivin' longhorns north to markets that still had money. They swapped their uniforms for dusters and their swords for ropes."

He gave a small nod.

"That's where Texas found her second wind, not in battle, but in work. The war was over, but the ridin' wasn't."

The old man reached for the lantern and blew it out. The porch fell dark, and the wind carried the last curl of smoke into the night.

CHAPTER ELEVEN

The Long Drives

When the Guns Went Quiet

The morning was still, just the hum of insects and the slow creak of the porch boards. The old man watched the first light spill over the pasture and warm the wet grass. For a long time, he said nothing. Then, in that voice worn thin by years, he started.

"When the war ended, Texas went quiet," he said. "No drums, no parades, just silence and the wind movin' across empty fields. The soldiers came home to dust, fences down, and cattle runnin' wild. Money was gone, but the land hadn't left us. The land never does."

He turned his hat in his hands, brushing a thumb along the brim.

"Everywhere you looked, there were longhorns, rangy, mean, and half-starved, wanderin' the prairie by the thousands. They were worth near nothin' here, but up north, a steer brought thirty dollars. A man with grit and a rope could see the arithmetic plain enough. The South was broke, but the North was hungry. All that stood between the two was a thousand miles of bad country."

He tapped his boot heel on the porch rail.

"That's when the trails began. Not out of glory, out of need. The war had taken most of the men's fight but left their horses and their nerve. They saddled up again, traded gray coats for dusters, rifles for lariats, and started pushin' beef instead of banners. Some called it foolish; others, salvation. It was both."

He looked toward the east, where the sun was pulling color out of the sky.

"The first drives were rough. Herds of longhorns that hadn't seen a fence or a hand since before the war. They'd stampede at a whisper. Rivers had to be crossed one at a time, and rustlers waited on both banks. The men were mostly veterans, soldiers, freedmen, Tejanos, and boys who'd grown up too fast. They rode together because hunger don't ask about the color of a man's coat."

He poured himself a little coffee, the steam catching the light.

"By sixty-six the word had spread, beef for the takin' if you could get it north. Trails formed like wagon ruts across the plains: the **Chisholm**, the **Western**, the **Goodnight-Loving**. Some headed for Abilene, some for Dodge, some clear to Colorado. A trail boss might earn a hundred dollars a month for a drive that could last half a year. The cowhands made thirty a month, if they made it home at all."

He smiled faintly.

"My granddaddy used to say those men were half dust and half prayer. They slept under the stars, drove all day, and sang to the cattle at night to keep 'em calm. Simple songs, low and steady, the kind that sound like the wind. Folks who never rode the trail think of cowboys as heroes. Truth is, they were workin' men on borrowed horses."

He rose from the chair and leaned a hand on the post.

"Texas was still hurtin', but the cattle drives gave her a reason to breathe again. Every herd that reached the railhead put coin back in a country that had near forgotten what it looked like. Out of ruin came trade, and out of work came pride. We'd been fightin' to prove ourselves for twenty years. Now we just wanted to eat."

The boy nodded slowly, eyes on the horizon.

"So that's how it started," the old man said. "A broke land, a wild herd, and a handful of men too stubborn to quit. The guns were quiet, but the hooves had started talkin'. You could hear 'em clear to Kansas."

He set his hat back on his head and smiled a little.

"Next we'll talk about those riders, the drovers, the vaqueros, the freedmen, and the boys who found their manhood somewhere between a campfire and a stampede."

The old man stepped down off the porch, scuffing his heel against the dirt. "Every drive had its leaders," he said. "Men who knew the land, the cattle, and how to stay alive long enough to make it pay. Names that still mean somethin' when the wind's right, **Goodnight**, **Loving**, **Chisholm**."

He looked out across the pasture, where the grass waved gold in the morning sun.

"**Charles Goodnight** was a Ranger once, before the war. He had a knack for keepin' men together and cattle movin'. **Oliver Loving** was older, quieter, but just as tough. In sixty-six, they joined up to drive herds west to the Army forts in New Mexico and north to Colorado. Folks thought they were crazy, headin' into country ruled by the Comanche, Kiowa, and worse. But they went anyway. Hunger'll make a man brave."

He brushed a hand across his chin, eyes far away.

"They rode out from the Concho River with eighteen men and more than two thousand head. It was hot as the devil's kitchen, dust thick enough to choke a wagon team. When they reached the **Pecos**, Loving rode ahead with one hand and a few Mexican cowhands to make a deal for beef. Goodnight told him not to go, said the river bends were full of Comanche sign, but Loving was hard to turn. He figured speed was safer than delay."

The old man leaned a shoulder against the porch post.

"He made it a good way before they found him. Comanche came on 'em near a dry gulch west of **Fort Sumner**. They fired an arrow into Loving's leg and left him trapped in a shallow wash, hidin' in the heat for two days with nothin' but warm water and grit. When a settler found him, he was half gone. The doctors cut the leg, but the fever stayed. Before he died, he sent word to Goodnight."

He looked down, thumb rubbin' slow across his palm.

"They say the message was simple. 'Bring me home.' That's all. And Goodnight did. He loaded his friend's body into a wagon filled with salt, hauled him back across five hundred miles of desert and plains, and buried him in **Weatherford,** Texas, the first man laid to rest in what became known as the Goodnight-Loving Trail. Two cowmen keepin' their word, that's how Texas was built."

He reached for the coffeepot, poured a swallow, and sat on the step instead of the chair.

"Then there was **Jesse Chisholm**, part Cherokee, part Scot, all trader. His trail ran from the **Red River** to **Abilene, Kansas**. It started as a trade route and became the lifeline of the drives. You could follow his wagon ruts north and find pieces of Texas all along it, herds, songs, and men lookin' for one more payday. They called it the **Chisholm Trail**, but truth was, it belonged to every drover who ever followed dust and thunder north."

He shifted his hat back and nodded toward the horizon.

"Those herds were wild longhorns, raw-boned, mean, horns wide as wagon tongues. The men who handled 'em were the same kind. They'd ride two thousand head from the **Brazos** to Kansas, sleepin' in the open and eatin' what the cook could scrape together. Beans, bacon, sour bread, and coffee so strong it'd make your teeth holler."

He smiled faintly.

"The herds could run at a whisper. A clap of thunder, a light too sudden, and the ground itself would move. Stampedes could last half the night. The men would sing to calm the cattle, slow, soft songs with more dust than melody. Bury Me Not on the Lone Prairie, The Old Chisholm Trail, and others lost to memory. I reckon it wasn't just for the cattle. Singin' gave a man somethin' to hold on to while the stars looked down and counted his mistakes."

He looked at the boy.

"You ever heard of trail towns? Abilene, Dodge, Newton, they started as dots on a map and grew up mean. Every drive ended there, and so did most of the men's wages. The cowhands would ride in with months of dust in their hair, pockets full of pay, and a thirst that couldn't wait. By sunrise, the money was gone, and they were already talkin' about the next drive."

The boy frowned. "Didn't they ever stop?"

The old man laughed once, short and dry.

"No more than the wind does. A few bought land, built ranches, and tried to settle. Most just kept ridin'. They said the trail gets in your blood. You follow it long enough, and you start hearin' hooves even in your sleep."

He paused and rubbed the side of his neck.

"The trail hands were every kind, white, Black, Mexican, Indian. "Freedmen rode right alongside old soldiers one in three cowboys was a freedman," the old man said. "Vaqueros showed green boys how to throw a rope and stay in the saddle. Out there, nobody asked where you came from. A man's worth was in his hands, and how he handled himself when the herd went bad. The trail didn't care about color or names. It only cared if you could hold on."

He looked out at the pasture again, where the sun was risin' high and the air shimmered with heat.

"Those years after the war were lean, but the drives gave Texas a way to stand again. Beef to the north, coin to the south, and pride somewhere in between. It was hard work, dirty work, but it built somethin' that lasted longer than the glory of any battle. Work's the only victory that don't fade."

He got up, brushed the dust from his hands, and set his hat on his head.

"Next, we'll ride with 'em up those trails, across rivers, through storms, and into towns that barely remembered their own names. You'll see what it costs to move Texas north one hoof at a time."

The Trails North

The old man pushed his hat back and stared north, where the haze lay low and flat.

"Most of the herds that left Texas took one of three trails," he said. "The **Chisholm**, the **Goodnight-Loving**, or, later, the **Western**. The Chisholm was the busiest, a river of horns and dust. You could follow it from the **Red River** clear up through Indian Territory to **Abilene** and **Dodge City, Kansas**. The others ran lonelier, stretchin' west through New Mexico or up the high plains toward **Ogallala, Nebraska**. Didn't matter which you took, every mile carried the same song of wind, sweat, and hooves."

He shifted his weight and leaned on the porch post.

"Crossin' a river was always the hardest. "The Brazos, the Red, the Canadian, even the small creeks, looked gentle till you tried pushin' two thousand head across. Cattle hate movin' water. You could holler and wave till your throat went raw, and they'd still bunch up on the bank. When one slipped, a few more followed, and before long the whole herd was thrashin'. You'd see horns, foam, and a man or two fightin' to stay on top. Nothin' quiets a camp faster than a river gone bad."Some men never came up, and the ones who did carried that sound with 'em for the rest of their lives."

He took a long breath.

"Storms were worse. The plains could turn mean in a heartbeat, a blue sky one minute, a black one the next. I've heard stories of lightnin' hittin' the herd and killin' fifty head in one flash. When the thunder rolled, the herd didn't think, it just ran. Dust, hooves, and fear all mixed together.

A man could lose his horse or his life in a blink. The hands would swing into the saddle, ridin' the edge and singin' low, tryin' to bring the herd back to its senses. Sometimes it was a hymn, sometimes a tune they made up on the spot. Didn't matter what they said, just that the cattle heard a calm voice in the storm." Didn't matter. It was the voice that steadied the herd."

He rubbed the back of his neck, his fingers slow and deliberate.

"Stampedes were the worst thing a man could face. The ground itself trembled. You'd lose the sky, the trail, and any sense of direction. You just hung on. When it stopped, there was always silence, no breathin', no cryin', just the smell of dirt and blood. And then you'd start again, because the herd didn't care what you'd lost."

He picked up the tin cup, swirled the coffee, and drank.

"Every trail had a code. The cook was king; you didn't cross him. The horse wrangler got the first coffee because he had to be gone before daylight. The trail boss didn't yell; he didn't have to. A look from him carried more weight than a sermon. When a man died, the crew buried him on high ground, his boots on and his hat over his face. They marked the grave with a rock and kept ridin'. The herd couldn't wait for grief."

He smiled faintly.

"The cook's wagon was the heart of every drive. He was doctor, barber, banker, and preacher rolled into one.

When the fire was lit and the beans were boilin', the camp turned into a kind of home, rough, but steady. The coffee was thick as tar and twice as bitter, but it kept the ghosts away. They said if the chuck wagon was still standin' come morning, the world wasn't done with you yet."

The boy looked up from his notes, "Did they all make it back?"

The old man shook his head. He took a moment; his eyes fixed on the horizon.

"Some couldn't. Fever, river crossings, bullets, the trail had a hundred ways to take a man. But those who made it home had somethin' no one could buy. They'd seen the edge of the world and come back with dust in their blood. They called themselves cowboys, though the name didn't matter then. They were just men who'd traded fear for distance."

He pushed the hat down over his brow.

"When they hit the Kansas railheads, the noise changed, from hooves to piano music and gunfire. **Abilene**, **Dodge**, Ellsworth, towns that smelled of whiskey, sweat, and new money. The drovers would roll in, pockets full and hearts empty. They'd buy drinks, gamble, fight, laugh, and forget. By dawn, most of it was gone, the money, the bruises, and half their pride. But come spring, they'd ride again."

He paused, voice softer now.

"Those towns had their own kind of danger. A man could survive stampedes and drownin' rivers, then die in a barroom fight over a hand of cards. But that's the trail's way, she takes what she wants, and she don't ask."

He looked down at his hands, rough from years that still felt close.

"The trail taught Texas more than work. It taught patience, courage, and how to start over. It gave us back our backbone after the war took it. And when those herds thundered north, they carried more than beef, they carried the sound of a state learnin' to breathe again."

He leaned back in his chair, the boards moaning under his weight.

"By the time the last herd reached Kansas, the dust hung so thick folks said the sun looked red for a week. But that dust was the color of rebirth. It meant Texas was alive."

He nodded toward the boy.

"Next comes how it ended, barbed wire, railroads, and fences that cut the world down to size. The open range didn't die with a gunshot, boy. It just ran out of sky."

CHAPTER TWELVE

Blood and Dust on the Frontier

The Last Riders

The light was low, the kind that turns the grass gray before dark. The old man sat still for a long time, listening to the wind settle down and the night start to wake. When he spoke, his voice came slow and even, the way men talk when they've run out of hurry.

"After the drives ended," he said, "the land got quiet again. The cowhands drifted to towns or ranches, and the Rangers went home. But the frontier wasn't done. It just changed hands. The soldiers came after the Civil War, blue coats and brass buttons, ridin' where the old trails had faded. They called it bringin' order. We called it another kind of fight."

He took off his hat, brushed the brim with his thumb, and set it on the rail.

"The forts came first. You could follow 'em like mile markers across the map, stone posts, wooden barracks, and log stockades stretchin' from the Red River to the Rio Grande. They said they were there to protect settlers, stage lines, and telegraph wires. Truth was, they were there to finish the job the Rangers had started: to tame what was left of the wild country."

He leaned forward, elbows resting on his knees.

"I remember my grandfather talkin' about ridin' near Fort Richardson, near Jacksboro. Said the bugles sounded thin against all that emptiness. The soldiers drilled, cleaned rifles, and wrote letters home about heat and loneliness. They fought boredom more than battles, but when the trouble came, it came hard."

He rubbed his hands together as though he could still feel the grit of that country.

"The forts were a long way apart," he said. "Just lonely places stuck out in the wind. Griffin, Concho, Davis, you could ride for days and never see one from the next. Out there, it was all sky, all grass. The soldiers did their drills, blew their bugles, and tried to act like the world cared. It didn't. The land never saluted anybody. Most nights they slept in their boots, guns close by, hopin' they'd hear trouble before it found 'em." Some nights they slept with their boots on, rifles close, knowin' a war party might pass through the dark before the guards ever caught sight of it." Other times, they rode for weeks and never saw a soul."

He looked toward the boy.

"Most of the soldiers were young, many of 'em colored, the Buffalo Soldiers. Hard men who'd seen too much fightin' back east and still signed on to guard a country that barely claimed 'em. The plains didn't care about skin color, and neither did the bullets. They did their duty just the same. Folks didn't always thank 'em for it, but they were as good a soldier as the frontier seen."

The boy nodded. "Did they ever meet the Rangers?"

The old man smiled a little.

"Now and again. The Rangers were older then, runnin' scouts or actin' as guides. The Army had numbers and supplies; the Rangers had the know-how. Between 'em, they made a hard team to beat. The Comanche and Kiowa called the soldiers the long knives' and the Rangers 'wolf riders.' Either way, they meant trouble."

He picked up the pipe, turned it in his hand, and tapped it empty against his boot heel.

"By the late sixties, the fights were gettin' fewer but sharper. The tribes were still raiding, not for conquest, but for survival. The settlers kept pushin' west, and the soldiers kept followin'. Texas was growin' bigger in name and smaller in spirit. You could feel the end comin', even if no one wanted to say it."

He set the pipe aside, the bowl gleaming faintly in the lamplight.

"That's where we are now, boy. The last riders on the last frontier. The Army posts, the Buffalo Soldiers, the scouts, and the Rangers still ridin' because they didn't know how to quit. The wind carried their bugles clear across the plains, echoing off canyons that hadn't heard silence in a hundred years."

He looked out toward the horizon, where the night had swallowed the last of the day.

"It wasn't glory anymore. It was cleanup, the long, slow end of the world the tribes had built, and the settlers couldn't understand. But the soldiers did their job, and Texas called it peace. Every victory left the land a little emptier."

The old man rose, straightened his back, and reached for the lantern.

"Let's talk next about those forts, and the men who lived and died in 'em. You'll see what it took to hold a country together when the ground itself didn't want taming."

The Fort Line

The old man rested both hands on the porch rail, the lantern glow catching the dust in the air.

"After the war," he said, "the U.S. Army came west and started nailin' the frontier down with forts. They didn't ask the land's permission. Just started buildin'. You can follow their bones across a map like a trail of worry, stone, timber, and sweat stretched from the Red River clear to the Rio Grande."

He drew a line in the dust with his boot.

"The first posts went up in the forties, Fort Graham, Fort Croghan, Fort Inge, Fort Clark, Fort Gates, small wooden stockades built close to water and far from help. When the settlers kept movin' west, the forts moved too. By the time Texas had joined the Union again, the army was buildin' a second wall of posts farther out, bigger, stronger, made to last. People think all the old forts had walls but those built around them were usually just buildings in a square, barracks and officers' quarters, with a hospital close by"

He ticked them off on his fingers.

"Fort Richardson just south of Jacksboro. Fort Griffin on the Clear Fork of the Brazos. Fort Concho near San Angelo, dead center of the state. Fort Davis down in the mountains, Fort Stockton on the desert road, and Fort Clark guardin' the southern crossings. Fort Phantom Hill, north of Abilene was a fort before the war, but only a camp when the blue soldiers returned. Every one of 'em a small patch of law surrounded by miles of silence. The soldiers called it a line of defense. The tribes weren't so pleasing."

He took off his hat and fanned himself with it.

"Inside those posts were men who'd fought the big war back east and boys who'd never seen a fight at all. The 4th U.S. Cavalry were white troopers, but the10th Cavalry, 9th Cavalry, 24th and 25th Infantry, they made up the most numbers…white officers and Black troopers who came to be known as the Buffalo Soldiers. Hard soldiers, tougher than rawhide. The name came from the Plains tribes, out of respect more than insult. They said the soldiers' hair and courage both reminded 'em of the buffalo they hunted."

He sat down, the old chair complaining under him.

"Those men did the worst jobs the army had. They chased raiders, guarded mail stages, strung telegraph wire, hauled water, and buried their own. They were paid less, supplied worse, and worked in places nobody else wanted. Out at Fort Davis, they patrolled the Davis Mountains, escortin' wagon trains through Apache country. At Fort Stockton, they guarded the San Antonio–El Paso road, watchin' for bandits and the Mescalero Apaches crossin' from Mexico. Farther north, the Buffalo Soldiers of Fort Concho and Fort Griffin rode endless circles around ranches that barely existed yet."

He looked toward the pasture.

"Fort Richardson became the heart of it all. From there rode Colonel Ranald Mackenzie and his Fourth Cavalry, young, sharp, and mean as a winter storm. In the summer of seventy-four, he gathered troops from Fort Concho and Fort Griffin and marched north into the Panhandle. They followed Comanche and Kiowa trails across the Llano Estacado till they dropped into Palo Duro Canyon. That canyon's deep enough to hide a whole nation. The villages were there, hundreds of lodges, food stores, and near fifteen hundred horses. Mackenzie's men hit 'em at dawn, burned the lodges, and shot the horses so they couldn't be taken back. It broke the tribes' legs, figuratively and for real. They never moved the same after that."

He turned the cup in his hand, the tin rasping on the boards.

"Fort Griffin was where the scouts came from. Tonkawa men, mostly, old enemies of the Comanche, along with Black Seminole Scouts out of Fort Clark. They were the best trackers the army ever had, could read a trail like a printed page. Officers might get the glory, but those scouts did the findin' and the dyin'."

He paused, thinking, and continued, "Fort Concho handled the supply trains, wagons haulin' corn, beans, and rifle rounds across country that could kill a team in a day. The wagons were strung out for miles, each wheel creakin' like a groan. A lot of those waggoners were civilians, Mexican Teamsters and freedmen, fightin' heat, dust, and ambushes just to keep the army fed."

He drew on his pipe but didn't light it.

"Out west, Fort Davis was the loneliest of 'em all. High stone walls, cool nights, and the kind of quiet that can make a man forget his own name. The Tenth Cavalry held it down, ridin' after Apache bands that slipped across the border. A patrol might be gone three weeks and come back with nothing to show but worn horses and sunburnt faces."

He looked at the boy.

"Fort Clark down south watched the Rio Grande. The Seminole Negro Scouts worked from there, crossin' the river in silence, huntin' bandits and raiders. They wore pieces of old uniforms and carried Sharps carbines. When they came back, they'd ride straight to the corrals, water the horses, and go back out again before the dust had settled."

The boy frowned. "So many forts. Did it work?"

The old man thought a moment.

"Depends on what you call work," he said. "They made the country safe enough for wagons and cattle, sure. But every fort meant one more nail in the coffin for the people who'd called this land theirs. The soldiers built fences out of discipline and patrol routes, not wire. They weren't bad men, most of 'em, just doin' what they were told. But every bugle note pushed the wild a little farther west."

He tapped his pipe gently on the rail.

"Those posts were small towns of their own. Each had a parade ground, a bakery, a hospital, and a grave-yard. The graveyards always filled first. Some were soldiers, some scouts, some women and children who tried to make homes behind those walls. The wind still hums through their markers."

He turned to the boy, eyes steady.

"By the seventies, the fort line stretched clean across Texas. You could ride from Fort Clark to Fort Richardson and never be out of sight of the army's work, even if it was only just a supply road. When Mackenzie broke the last stronghold at Palo Duro, the fighting spirit of the plains tribes started to fade. But it didn't end quick. You can't break a people overnight."

He stood, stretching his back till it popped.

"Those soldiers, white and Black alike, paid their dues out there. Heat, hunger, and ambush. They didn't win glory; they just outlasted everyone else."

He set the cup down, the sound hollow in the quiet.

"That's what the fort line really was, time made into walls. The army called it progress. The land called it the beginning of the end."

He nodded toward the horizon.

"Next we'll talk about who they were fightin', the Comanche and Kiowa, how their bands worked, and what it meant to live free under that big, empty sky."

The People of the Plain

The night had grown quiet except for the hum of crickets in the grass. The old man took a slow pull of coffee and stared out toward the west, where the stars lay thick and close together.

"The army called it the Indian problem," he said. "But it wasn't a problem. It was a people. The Comanche and Kiowa weren't fightin' to win new land; they were fightin' to keep what had always been theirs. That's what the forts and the soldiers never understood."

He leaned forward, elbows on his knees.

"The Comanche Nation was never a single tribe like the books try to tell it. It was a family of five great bands, each with its own chiefs, council, and hunting grounds. The Penateka were the southern branch, the ones who met Austin's settlers first. They traded with both the Mexicans and the Texans, and they carried the weight of all the early peace talks. The Nokoni and Kotsoteka held the middle plains , strong riders, raiders when they had to be. The Yamparika ranged up north along the Canadian River, always on the move, never far from the buffalo. And the Quahada, the western band, were the last and hardest to find, proud horsemen, pure plains people, led in the end by Quanah Parker, who carried both Comanche blood and settler eyes."

He drew a small circle in the dust with his boot.

"Each band had its own way. The camps were laid out like little towns," he said. "Families kept close The women handled the hides and the fires. The old men taught the boys what to notice, How the wind shifted, what the clouds were sayin', the way grass bends when it's time to move camp. The chiefs weren't kings, not even close. Folks followed the ones they trusted. A man earned that by doin' right, sometimes through bravery, sometimes just by takin' care of people. It wasn't about speeches. You showed it, or you didn't. Words didn't mean much unless a man had the deeds to back 'em. Raids weren't about hate or conquest, they were the same as any hunt: a way to provide, to test yourself, to keep the young men sharp."

He rubbed his hands together slowly.

"The heart of their world was the buffalo. That animal gave them everything, food, shelter, clothes, tools, even music. The hides became lodges and robes: the sinew, thread for bowstrings, and sewing. Horns turned into spoons and cups. The bones were made into knives, scrapers, needles, and toys for the children. The stomach became a water bag. The tail was a fly whisk or a child's rattle. Nothing went to waste. Even the dung was fuel, burnin' hot and clean on cold nights when there wasn't a stick of wood to be found. Every kill was a ceremony, gratitude first, meat second. They said each herd carried its own spirit, and a hunter had to speak to it before he drew the bow."

He sat back and let out a long breath.

"When the herds moved, the whole world moved with 'em. "If you climbed a hill and looked out," he said, "you'd see dark shapes coverin' the whole horizon, buffalo, thousands of 'em, movin' steady like water. The ground shook under your boots, and the air buzzed with the sound. Hunters rode in close, bareback and fast, lettin' arrows fly before the herd even knew they were there. The horses trusted their riders, and the riders trusted the wind to carry 'em through." When it was done, there'd be laughter, prayers, smoke, and meat for the winter. That was life, simple, balanced, and right."

He paused, running a hand along the brim of his hat.

"The Kiowa shared that life. Smaller in number but just as proud. They were travelers and poets, kept histories in drawings and songs. Their calendar sticks marked the years by great hunts or winters of suffering. They rode with the Comanche, married into their bands, and shared the same enemies. The Kiowa-Apache and their allies spoke another tongue but followed the same trail. Between them, they ruled a country larger than any one nation on paper. From the Arkansas River in the north to the Rio Grande in the south, they could move in any direction and never feel like strangers."

He sipped his coffee and set it down on the porch rail.

"They weren't savages. They were specialists, masters of horses, trade, and diplomacy. They traded buffalo hides for Spanish iron, swapped horses for Mexican silver, and took captives to sell or ransom. Every raid had a purpose. Some for revenge, some for wealth, some to count coup, a mark of bravery. Their wealth was in horses; their pride was in skill. A good hunter could feed a camp of fifty. A brave warrior could protect them all."

He rubbed the pipe bowl between his palms.

"Life out there wasn't easy, but it was full. The women ran the camps, tanned the hides, cooked the food, and kept the families strong. The old men told stories by firelight, of creation, of the buffalo's gift, of how the stars were once people who climbed into the sky. Every story was a map of gratitude. They didn't think they owned the land. They thought they belonged to it."

He turned his eyes toward the boy.

"You take away the buffalo, and you take away that world. That's what happened. When the herds started vanishin' in the early seventies, it wasn't just hunger that came. It was grief, deep and quiet. The tribes watched the horizon and saw smoke from white hunters' fires. The Sharps rifles could drop a buffalo from half a mile. They shot 'em by the hundreds, stripped the hides, and left the carcasses to rot. The smell carried for miles. What had once been sacred became waste. It was like killin' a church every day."

He leaned forward, voice lower now.

"The Comanche said the buffalo were their older brothers, the first people made by the Creator. When the hunters left the plains covered in bones, the medicine men said the world had been turned upside down. They were right. Without the herds, there was no food, no trade, no reason to move. The children starved. The warriors sold their horses to buy flour and blankets. The women wept for more than hunger; they wept for the silence. The ground didn't thunder anymore. The song of life was gone from it."

He looked down at his hands, calloused and rough.

"The army didn't understand they were already fightin' ghosts. The battles that came later, the canyon raids, the last surrenders, those were echoes of a world already dyin'. When the buffalo fell, the Comanche and Kiowa lost the heartbeat of who they were. All that was left was memory."

He looked up, eyes steady but tired.

"I've heard folks say the plains were empty before we came. That's a lie told by people who never understood. The plains were full of hooves, prayers, laughter, and the breath of a people who knew how to live with the land instead of against it. If you stand out there on a still night, you can feel it. The air still remembers the herd, and maybe it remembers the Comanche too."

He turned down the lantern wick, and the light sank low.

"That's who the army rode against, boy, not savages, but a nation of horsemen bound to the buffalo. The next fights were their last, the ones that broke the circle for good. You'll hear about that next,about the canyon where the soldiers came at dawn, and the man who walked out of the ashes to end a war that should never have started."

The Final Campaigns: Palo Duro and Beyond

The old man eased back in the chair, boots hitting the boards with a soft knock.

"By the early seventies," he began, "the fightin' was smaller, but it cut deeper. The buffalo were about gone, and the tribes were hangin' on to what little they had left. Every raid felt like it might be the last one. Out near Jacksboro, the army found out what that kind of desperation costs."

He lifted his hat and wiped a line of sweat from his brow.

"It was May of seventy-one. A freight line called Warren's Wagon Train was movin' goods between the forts, Richardson and Griffin, when a Kiowa war party came down on 'em along Salt Creek Prairie, about twenty miles west of here. The teamsters never had a chance. They were outnumbered ten to one, maybe worse. Seven men died before the smoke cleared, wagons burned, mules run off. The army buried what was left and sent word back east that peace was done."

He picked up the tin cup, turned it once, then set it aside.

"That raid lit a fire under Washington. The government said the frontier had to be quieted once and for all. Colonel Mackenzie's Fourth Cavalry, ridin' out of Fort Richardson, got the order to take the field. The Kiowa chiefs Satanta, Big Tree, and Satank were blamed for the attack. Satanta bragged about it to a reservation agent; he couldn't help himself. That brag cost him. The army arrested him and the others, marched 'em in irons to Jacksboro, and put 'em on trial."

He rubbed the bridge of his nose, remembering the stories.

"It was the first time the government ever tried Indian leaders in a civil court. The crowd in Jacksboro wanted hangin's. Satank tried to escape on the way to trial, sang his death song, and went down fightin'. Satanta and Big Tree were sentenced to death, but the governor commuted it to life. They'd spend their years behind stone walls instead of under an open sky. Satanta couldn't take being apart from the land, grew sadder each day, until he took his own life. That trial and what followed told everyone what was comin'. The age of treaties was over; the age of orders had begun."

He looked toward the dark fields stretching north.

"Two years later, Mackenzie rode again. This time it wasn't about punishment. It was about endings. The Red River War of 1874 brought every soldier in Texas to bear. Mackenzie's Fourth, Buffalo Soldiers from the Ninth and Tenth Cavalry, scouts from the Tonkawa and Black Seminoles, all of 'em movin' north out of Fort Concho, Fort Richardson, and Fort Griffin. They were told to find the villages, burn the stores, kill the horses, and force the tribes onto the reservation. It was ugly work, but they did it."

He set his hat on his knee, his voice slow and even.

"The worst of it came that fall, deep in the Palo Duro Canyon. That canyon's wide as a river and near three hundred feet down, carved clean through the Caprock by wind and water. The Kiowa, Comanche, and Cheyenne thought they were safe there, with their winter lodges, food caches, and herds tucked in the canyon's bends. Mackenzie's scouts found the trail down. At dawn, the soldiers dropped into the canyon like ghosts. They hit fast, burnin' lodges, takin' supplies, scatterin' families into the brush. Then they rounded up more than a thousand horses, the last strength of the plains, and shot every dadgum one of 'em."

He paused and stared at the cup still sitting on the rail.

"Some said it was cruel. Maybe it was. But Mackenzie knew what he was doin'. You take away a Comanche's horse, you take away his life. The tribes that got out of that canyon walked back to the reservation at Fort Sill hungry and beaten. The rest never left the plains. The army called it victory. The tribes called it the death of the wind."

He stood and walked to the edge of the porch.

"It didn't stop right then. Skirmishes still broke out along the Canadian and the Staked Plains. Mackenzie kept ridin', chasin' small bands that tried to hold on. The Buffalo Soldiers stayed on patrol, men from Fort Concho watchin' the San Saba, others from Fort Clark ridin' the Rio Grande trail. The work was endless, thankless, and hard. But by seventy-five, the last free Comanche band, the Quahada, came in. They rode into Fort Sill behind their chief, Quanah Parker. He'd been raised in both worlds, son of Cynthia Ann Parker, taken from Fort Parker long years before. He was the last chief to surrender, and the first to understand that fightin' any longer would only bring more graves."

He rubbed his jaw, the motion slow and thoughtful.

"After Palo Duro, the buffalo were gone. The hunters had seen to that. The plains that once thundered under a million hooves turned quiet. Bone pickers came after, loadin' wagons with what was left. The soldiers had their orders, the settlers had their land, and the people who'd called the plains home had nothin' left to follow."

He looked at the boy.

"The army didn't win by battle. It won by patience and numbers. The forts were its hands, reachin' farther each year until there was no place left to hide. The men who rode those campaigns, Mackenzie, the Buffalo Soldiers, the scouts, they did what they thought was right. Some of 'em even respected the people they fought. But right or wrong, they ended a world."

The old man sat back down, the chair sighing under his weight.

"Quanah Parker lived out his days near Cache Creek in Oklahoma, buildin' a big house with windows and doors like any rancher. He wore a suit to Washington, shook hands with presidents, invested in a railroad, and still prayed to the sun every morning. Folks said he carried peace like a burden. Maybe he did. He was proof that courage ain't tied to a uniform."

He took a slow breath, the kind that comes from deep memory. He rubbed his jaw before speaking.

"Up north, that Red River fight was the last bad one," he said. "After it, well... things just shifted. The wind still blew, but you heard dust in it instead of horses. The forts quieted down. A few of the Rangers started wearin' badges. The blue-coat soldiers drifted off to other places, and the ground they'd fought overturned into farms before most folks even paid it any mind." You can stand out there today and still see the shape of the canyon, but the sound's gone. Only the wind remembers."

He turned toward the boy. "That's how the frontier ended, not with glory, but with tired men ridin' home and the tribes walkin' north to a different kind of prison. There were no winners. Just survivors."

He looked down at his hands, then out into the dark.

"The soldiers went back to their forts. The Comanche went back to the dust. And Texas moved on, proud and restless as ever."

He drew in one last breath of the cool night air and nodded.

"Next time, we'll talk about what came after, the forts turnin' into towns, the windmills and fences, and how Texas finally grew quiet. Took a hundred years, but the land never forgets what it cost."

The Quiet Frontier

The old man stayed quiet for a spell. The lantern between them burned low, throwing just enough light to make shadows dance. Somewhere out in the dark, a coyote called once and quit.

He cleared his throat before speaking. "When the shootin' stopped and the herds were gone, Texas didn't feel the same. The forts turned into towns. The soldiers traded their rifles for ledgers. The scouts, well, they turned into stories.. You can still find the old parade grounds if you know where to look, patches of flat earth where the grass grows short, maybe a bit of stone left from a wall. The wind whistles through those ruins like it's countin' ghosts."

He rubbed his hands together slowly.

"The buffalo were near gone by then. A few hunters still worked the northern plains, gatherin' bones to sell by the ton. Folks back east made fertilizer and china from what used to feed a continent. The land that once moved like a tide had gone still. Only the bones stayed, white as the moonlight."

He tipped his hat back, eyes on the horizon he couldn't see.

"Some men couldn't stand to see it end. Charles Goodnight was one of those. He'd run cattle, fought Indians, and seen more than his share of death. When the killing stopped, he kept a few buffalo alive down in the Palo Duro country, the last of their kind on Texas ground. He said somebody had to remember what they looked like."

The boy leaned forward. "Did they live?"

The old man nodded.

"For a time. There's an old story, might be true, might not. They say one day, a handful of Comanche rode up to Goodnight's place and asked if they could have some of his buffalo. He agreed, and they drove three head out onto the prairie. The men rode alongside, quiet at first. "They say the riders let out a cry you could feel in your chest," he said. "The buffalo bolted, and those men went with 'em, arrows flashin' in the sun. When it was done, all three animals were down in the dust. Goodnight just stood there, watchin'. Folks claim he had tears cuttin' lines through the trail dust on his face. Maybe he knew he'd just seen the last hunters bring down the last buffalo. Maybe that part's only talk. Still... it feels true, and it hurts to think on. But it sounds true enough to hurt."

He drew a breath that sounded close to a sigh.

"That was the end of an age, boy, not just for the buffalo or the Comanche, but for every soul that ever lived by the wind. The range was fenced, the rivers bridged, and the sky seemed smaller somehow. Texas had won her peace, but she'd buried her freedom with it."

He looked out across the dark pasture.

"The old forts crumbled. The bugles went quiet. The buffalo trails turned to wagon ruts, then to roads. The

Rangers took up law badges, and the soldiers marched away. What was left were the stories, and a land that still remembers."

He turned the lantern wick down until the flame sank to a glow.

"The land outlasts all of us," he said softly. It forgives slow, forgets slower. You can still feel the old ways under your boots if you walk far enough from the fences."

The boy didn't answer, just sat listening to the quiet. The old man smiled faintly, tired but at peace.

"Get some rest," he said. "Tomorrow's another story. The native wild's gone, but the wind's still talkin'."

He blew out the light. The porch went dark, and the sound of the wind moved through the grass, the same wind that once carried the thunder of hooves across an endless plain.

CHAPTER THIRTEEN

Hard Ground: Lawmen, Outlaws, and the Towns Between

After the Fences

The night had turned warm again, a still kind of heat that held the smell of dust and mesquite. The old man tilted his chair back, boots propped against the rail, eyes half closed. A moth beat against the lantern glass, thumping a slow rhythm.

The boy broke the quiet. "What happened after the buffalo were gone? After the forts?"

The old man's chair came down on all four legs. He looked at the boy for a moment, then at the dark yard beyond.

"When the fences went up," he said, "the wild didn't die. It just moved into town."

He set his hat on his knee, thumb running the brim slow.

"Texas was changin' fast. The range was cut up with barbed wire, the trails turned into wagon roads, and the big herds were mostly gone. But the men who'd rode that open country still had fight in 'em. They weren't made for quiet work. So they followed the cattle and the money to the new places sproutin' along the rail lines, Fort Worth, Dodge City, Tascosa, El Paso, San Antonio. Towns where a man could drink, gamble, and find trouble quicker than a prayer."

He gave a slight grin that didn't quite reach his eyes. "Those towns," he said, "they were young. Mean, too. Cowhands came in with pockets full of trail money. Gamblers were never far off, and the barkeeps poured whatever would burn goin' down. The law showed up late, if it showed at all. Nights got rough. Real rough. Lot of noise, bit of laughin', fights, and some poor piano bangin' away tryin' to drown it out." You'd hear pianos, folks shoutin', boots hittin' the boards, and now and then a gun go off somewhere down the street." Every one of 'em was tryin' to grow respectable while still smellin' like a saloon."

He picked up his coffee cup, found it empty, and set it back down.

"Fort Worth was called the end of the trail, the last stop before the cowhands returning from a drive, went home broke. Folks called its south side Hell's Half Acre. Gamblers like Luke Short and Bat Masterson ran the tables; Rangers walked the streets tryin' to keep the peace. It never lasted long. You could go to sleep to a fiddle tune and wake up to the sound of a coroner's wagon."

He looked out across the yard, the lantern light catchin' the lines in his face.

"Farther west, up on the Canadian River, there was Tascosa, the cowboy's graveyard. "It sat up there on the Panhandle trails, crossroads for every kind of drifter," he said. "Rangers, outlaws, hands lookin' for work, and women who didn't bother with questions. Saturday nights, the saloons spilled out into the street. By Sunday mornin', folks were mopin' up blood and broken glass. The sheriff used to say keepin' order there was like tryin' to herd cats with a stick."

He leaned forward, elbows on his knees.

"Every boomtown followed the same pattern, dust, money, blood, and regret. The drovers brought the dust, the gamblers took the money, the gunmen spilled the blood, and the rest of us were left with the regret. But it was a time that built Texas, same as the wars before it. A man had to stand for somethin' or he got swept under."

The boy frowned. "Was it that bad everywhere?"

The old man shook his head.

"Not everywhere, but close. The frontier didn't end clean, boy. It faded. The wild moved from the prairie to the streets, from the saddle to the saloon. There were lawmen, sure, but there were more ghosts than badges. Some folks made money, some made graves. The land wasn't fightin' anymore, the people were."

He straightened in his chair, voice softer now.

"That's what came after the fences, a hard breed of towns, rough men, and the law tryin' to catch up. It was the last gasp of the old Texas, and it came with piano music and gun smoke instead of war cries and thunder."

He reached for the lantern and turned it down just a little.

"Next, we'll walk through those towns, Tascosa, Fort Worth, El Paso, and the kind of men who gave 'em their stories. Some wore stars, some masks, and some didn't live long enough to take either one off."

Boomtowns and Bad Company

The old man poured a finger of cold coffee, took a sip, and grimaced. "You could tell when a town was about to turn mean," he said. "It smelled like money and gunpowder at the same time."

He looked out across the yard where fireflies blinked like tiny lanterns. "After the trails ended, the drovers and ranch hands drifted toward the railheads. A man used to ridin' herd all day needed somethin' to do with his hands and his pay. Towns sprang up fast, Fort Worth, Tascosa, El Paso, San Antonio, and a dozen more that barely lasted long enough to get on a map. Each one was built on dust, whiskey, and wishful thinkin'."

Fort Worth – Hell's Half Acre

"Fort Worth," he went on, "was the worst and proud of it. Folks called it the end of the trail and meant it. The south end of town was Hell's Half Acre, blocks of saloons, dance halls, and rooms rented by the hour. Drovers came in from the Chisholm Trail with six months' wages burnin' holes in their pockets. The barkeeps poured whiskey hot enough to blister paint, and the gamblers waited close. Luke Short ran cards there, same as Bat Masterson when Dodge City cooled off. Rangers walked the streets two at a time, hats low and hands close to their guns. The Acre never slept. Piano music, women laughin', somebody cursin', somebody prayin', all of it at once. Every morning, the undertaker swept the boardwalk clean again and got ready for nightfall."

He rubbed the side of his nose. "You could judge a saloon by its floorboards; sticky from drink meant business had been good, wet and blood red meant somebody didn't make it to the door. The law came late and usually limpin'. Sheriff Jim Courtright tried to tame it for a while, till Luke Short killed him in a gunfight so close they could've shaken hands before drawin'. Fort Worth learned respect after that, but not for long."

Tascosa – The Cowboy's Graveyard

He shifted in his chair till it quit squeaking. "Up north was a place called Tascosa," he said. "Sat out on the Canadian River, wind always blowin', dust so thick you could chew it. Folks called it the Panhandle's pride, and its curse. Every trail out of New Mexico seemed to run right through the middle of it." By sundown, the main street looked like a parade, Rangers, drifters, outlaws, gamblers, and cowhands lookin' for a drink or a fight. Saturday nights, the saloons overflowed, and by Sunday mornin' the town was sweepin' blood off its steps. The sheriff said tryin' to keep peace there was like stoppin' a tornado with a lariat."

He gave a dry laugh. "Tascosa had two things plenty of, guns and graves. Still, men came because they couldn't stand quiet. The sound of spurs on those boardwalks was like music to 'em. You can still find the cemetery out there, weather-beaten stones, half the names worn off. That ground tells more truth than any history book."

El Paso – The Border Town

He leaned his elbows on his knees. "El Paso sat down by the river and took in every kind of trouble the wind could blow in. It was half Texas, half Mexico, and all bad tempered. Smugglers, soldiers, and gamblers mixed together like whiskey and kerosene. The law didn't stick there long. A man named Dallas Stoudenmire wore the badge for a spell. tall fella, mean with a Colt. He cleaned up the town in one afternoon by killin' four men. Folks called it the 'Four Dead in Five Seconds Gunfight.' After that, he was respected and hated in equal parts. Didn't matter; somebody shot him in the back a few years later. El Paso was like that, justice didn't live long, but it died tryin'."

He tipped his hat back, eyes half-closed. "John Wesley Hardin ended his run there, too. He once bragged he had shot a man named Judge Moore for snorin'. Spent sixteen years in Huntsville Prison, came out wearin' a lawyer's coat and thinkin' the world owed him. A drunk and a bullet ended him in a saloon on San Antonio Street. They say the bartender swept up his hat with the glass."

San Antonio – Old Town, New Trouble

He drew a breath. "San Antonio had age on its missions, markets, soldiers, but it carried the same wild streak. Ben Thompson, gambler and gunfighter, called it home. He fought wars, ran saloons, and settled scores with lead. Got himself killed at the Vaudeville Theater, walked in laughin', carried out dead. Folks said he was smilin' when he hit the floor. That was the way of men like him. They burned bright and fast, and the city kept their ghosts."

The Women and the Rest

He rubbed his jaw before speaking again. "Weren't just men buildin' those towns," he said. "The women worked harder than most. Some kept boardin' houses, some cooked, some danced half the night just to stay fed. A few owned their own places, tough as rawhide, every one of 'em. Out west, near Abilene, there was a woman they called Big Nose Kate. She worked the saloons with Doc Holliday for a spell, then moved on. Hard life, but she lived it her way." In Tascosa, there was Molly Goodnight, settin' up a schoolhouse where nobody thought to ask for one. She used to say even the wildest land needed manners someday."

The Feel of a Town

"The sound of those places stays with you," he said. "Horses hittin' the boards, the rattle of dice, boots scrapin' on the floor. Nights smelled of smoke, perfume, and sweat. Mornings smelled of bleach and regret. The preachers came later, plantin' churches where saloons had burned. Every steeple in Texas stands on somebody's forgotten sin."

He chuckled once, low in his throat. "Money came easy if you didn't mind losin' your soul. A good gambler could make a month's wages in an hour, and a careless one could lose his boots before the cards were cold. Most of the sheriffs and marshals were former cowhands who just needed steady pay. The difference between the badge and the outlaw was usually which one the town could afford."

He took off his hat and wiped the sweatband with his thumb. "You asked how Texas got her backbone. This was it, these towns and the people in 'em. The law came slow, the order slower, but both came. Out of the noise and the drink and the blood, we learned what to keep and what to bury."

He looked toward the boy, a faint smile hiding in the wrinkles of his face. "Fort Worth, Tascosa, El Paso, San

Antonio, all of 'em still stand in some shape. You walk their streets now and see banks where the saloons were, courthouses where the jails stood. The ghosts are still there, though, sittin' in the doorways, waitin' for music that'll never start again."

He gave a faint grin that didn't last. "Those old towns still carry ghosts," he said. "You can feel 'em sittin' in the doorways, listenin' for music that ain't comin' back."

He bent forward, the chair creaking a little, or maybe it was his knee. These days, it was hard to tell, "Next part," he said. "We'll get to the ones tryin' to keep some kind of order. Rangers, sheriffs, whoever had the guts to stand up."

He rubbed his jaw, thinkin' a moment. "Folks call it law these days," he said. "Back then... it was mostly guesswork. Grit, maybe a bit of luck, that's all."

Badges and Blood

The old man took his hat off and laid it crown-down on the porch rail, thumb, flicking a piece of prairie grass from it as he sat it down.

"After the towns took root, somebody had to hold 'em together," he said. "Law was a slim thing back then, stretchin' from Austin clear to the border. Sometimes it snapped."

He tapped the rail twice, slowly. "The Rangers came back first. Not the same kind that'd ridden the plains before, but close enough. The state called 'em companies, A through D, and sent 'em where the trouble was thickest. Men like Leander McNelly down on the coast and John B. Jones up north. They didn't have much in the way of pay or mercy. McNelly's crew ran rustlers out of the Nueces Strip with gunfire for paperwork. Jones cleaned out the bandit camps in the hill country. They weren't saints. Just men with badges who shot straighter than most."

He looked at the boy. "McNelly died young. Consumption, they said. He'd spent too much of himself out in the brush. Folks still tell stories of him ridin' alone into outlaw camps, talkin' quiet till someone flinched. He'd come back with more holes in his coat than he left with. He never seemed to notice."

The old man reached for the coffeepot and poured a bit into his cup, more to give his hands something to do than a hankering for the brew. "The Rangers were the state's answer to chaos. Sometimes they fixed it. Sometimes they made it worse. Down south, they fought cattle thieves and smugglers. Along the border, they rode against Cortina's men, huntin' bandits one week and negotiatin' with 'em the next. Rangers fought for pay, for pride, and sometimes to prove they were the hardest men in the county."

He let the cup rest in his palm. "A lot of folks think the Rangers were always heroes. Truth is, they were human. Some kept the peace, some abused it. But they were what Texas had, and the land was still too wild to care how manners looked on a badge."

He looked off toward the yard. "Then came the sheriffs and town marshals, Jim Courtright in Fort Worth, Ben Thompson in Austin, Dallas Stoudenmire down in El Paso. Every one of 'em wore a gun for a reason. They knew that talk only lasted till the first man flinched. Courtright tried to bully Luke Short into payin' protection and caught two bullets for his trouble. Thompson shot his way through half of Austin before somebody finally got him from behind. Stoudenmire? Cleaned up El Paso, but his temper got him killed, just as it did the men he arrested. The law out here had a short life span."

He brushed a moth off the lantern glass. "Some Rangers turned bounty men when the state stopped payin'. A few joined posses for whoever could afford 'em. They'd chase bandits one month and guard cattle the next. The lines between law and outlaw blurred till you couldn't tell which side you were ridin' for."

The boy leaned forward a little. "Didn't anyone try to make real peace?"

The old man smiled, lips pursing together small and tired. "Peace wasn't the kind of thing you made back then, son. You just bought it for a while. A good sheriff could keep order till the next trail season, maybe longer if luck held. But the whiskey and the money always brought the wild back. It's the nature of people to test fences, same as cattle."

He picked up his hat again, turning it slowly in his hands. "Not all the Rangers rode for the state. Some stayed independents, workin' in little groups. One of 'em was Frank Hamer, just startin' out then. Young, quiet, mean as a snake when pushed. He'd go on to make his name later, but even then folks said he had a look that could stop a man mid-lie."

He looked down at the cup beside him. "Badges didn't mean protection. They meant responsibility. You wore one, you stood in front when the bullets came. And the bullets always came."

He gave a short laugh, more breath than sound. "There were times the law and the outlaws drank at the same table. They'd call a truce long enough to bury somebody, then go right back to shootin'. That was Texas in the eighties, half civilization, half chaos."

He set the hat back on his head. "Even the Rangers grew older, settled, turned into part of the government they used to ignore. They'd traded dust for desks, at least for a while. But the legend stuck, and folks still needed stories of men who could ride in and fix a thing with grit instead of speeches."

He looked at the boy, eyes soft under the shadow of his hat. "That's who they were, flawed, brave, stubborn men. They gave Texas its backbone, for better or worse."

The boy nodded. "What happened to the outlaws?"

The old man smiled faintly. "They come next. They always do. The bad men are easier to remember than the good ones. That's just the way stories work."

He tapped his cup once against the rail. "Next, we'll talk about 'em, Bass, Hardin, Belle Starr, and the rest. Folks called 'em legends. I call 'em lessons that came too late."

The Outlaws

The old man sat quiet for a while, watching the moths circle the lantern.

"Soon as folks built jails," he said, "other folks found reasons to fill 'em."

He took off his hat and brushed the crown with his palm.

"The war left boys mean and restless. It does something to some men, takes the good out of them. Oh, some tried farmin'. Most didn't last. Too much fight still in 'em. So they drifted to cards, whiskey, and easy money. That's how outlaws get made, not born, just worn down. Some taking an easier way than back breaking work or farming. Some things, like people, don't change."

He gave a short breath of laughter. "Sam Bass was one of 'em. Freight driver first. Got tired of slow pay. Started stoppin' trains instead of loadin' 'em. He used to brag that he never robbed the poor. Said the railroads could spare it. Sounded noble enough when he said it, but he kept most of the cash and spent what was left on horses and bad whiskey. Rangers ran him down near Round Rock in

'78. They hit him low, gutshot. He tried to smile, said somethin' about takin' his chance. Folks made a song after that. Songs always forget the part where a man bleeds out in the dirt."

He rubbed his hands together, slowly.

"Then there was Belle Starr, pretty name for a hard life. Rode with the Younger boys for a spell, kept company with Jesse James. Dressed fine, carried twin pistols, liked folks to notice. Papers called her the Bandit Queen, made her sound like a lady outlaw from a dime book. Truth is, she slept rough, ate worse, and trusted the wrong men. Somebody shot her from behind on a cold road up in Indian Territory. Never knew who. Maybe that's justice, maybe not."

He poured a finger of coffee, let it sit.

"John Wesley Hardin, he's the one folks still whisper about. Mean clear through. You heard how he killed a man for snorin'. That wasn't his worst sin. Hate lived in that man's bones. Carried it like other folks carry faith. Hated Yankees, hated freedmen, hated the world for movin' on without him. Claimed forty-two kills. Half that'd be too many. He told folks he never shot anyone who didn't need it. That was his excuse for bein' just plain mean'."

He looked down at his hands.

"They caught him back east, dragged him home in chains. Sixteen years in Huntsville didn't cure him none. When he got out, he put on a fancy coat and called himself a lawyer down in El Paso. Walked the streets like heaven had pardoned him. Still had snake eyes. Couldn't see the world had passed him by. One night, he mouthed off to a deputy, caught a bullet while throwin' dice. Fell right over the table. Folks said it was poetic. More like due payment for past sins."

He set the cup aside.

"Ben Thompson was another. Gambler, gun-hand, charmer when he felt like it. Could quote poetry one minute and shoot a man the next. Ran saloons in Austin, helped run 'em in San Antonio. Died in a theater lobby under gaslight, ambushed by men he'd already forgiven in his own mind. That's how quick grace runs out around here."

He looked toward the yard where the grass moved like shallow water.

"Jim Miller came later. Wore a preacher's coat, Bible in one hand, shotgun hid in the other. Worked for hire, killed folks for pay. Said the Lord understood his line of work. Maybe the Lord did; the jury didn't. The crowd pulled him out of jail and hanged him in Ada, Oklahoma. Four of 'em in the same necktie party. Somebody said he died smilin'. I don't buy it."

The chair creaked as he shifted his weight.

"Truth is, half the bad men you read about passed through Texas sooner or later. Jesse James, the Dalton boys, drifted close enough to smell the dust. The border gave 'em cover, and Texans gave 'em supper. We've always had a soft spot for folks who fight the rules, long as they don't fight us."

He gave a small shrug. "Some people liked 'em. Called 'em heroes, said they stood up to the big outfits. Folks love a story where the little man wins. The only thing is, these little men took from folks smaller than themselves. The papers left that part out. Makes for cleaner ink and better tales."

He ran a thumb along a nick in the rail.

"I met a fella once who'd known Bass. Said he was polite as a preacher till the shootin' started. Said he'd apologize after, like manners could fix a hole in your chest. That's how I think of the whole lot of 'em, apologies waitin' on graves."

He took off his hat and ran his fingers through his thin gray hair.

"You want the truth? None of those men were special. Just fast, and lucky till they weren't. They burned through their days and left the rest of us to sweep up."

He looked at the boy, eyes gone soft but steady.

"Stories make 'em larger. Songs make 'em saints. But the wind out on the prairie don't sing for 'em. It just moves the grass and forgets the names."

He leaned back, letting the chair creak.

"That's what time does, son. It forgets. Texas learned the hard way that courage without purpose turns to cruelty, and fame doesn't last any longer than gun smoke."

He rubbed a scar that cut across his palm.

"Those outlaws are dust now. The lawmen who chased 'em are dust, too. What's left is the land, and the stories we tell when the night gets quiet."

He glanced toward the dark pasture.

"Next, we'll talk about that quiet, the years when the guns rusted, the towns settled, and Texas tried on somethin' new: peace."

CHAPTER FOURTEEN

The Cattle Barons, The Empire of Dust and Brand

The Grass Kings

The evening train had rolled past a little earlier, but its echo still hung in the air, a low hum you could almost mistake for thunder. The old man sat quietly for a bit, pipe in hand, eyes on the dark horizon.

"Used to be," he said, "that sound you'd hear at dusk wasn't iron wheels. It was hooves, hundreds of 'em, maybe thousands, a herd movin' slow, dust hangin' in the sky like smoke from a grass fire. The trail herds were the blood of Texas back then, flowin' north toward the markets. But time moves faster than a man thinks. The drives ended, the fences came, and what used to belong to the wind started belongin' to brands."

He looked toward the boy. "That's when the **barons** came. The grass kings, they called 'em. Men who thought in miles instead of acres, who built kingdoms out of cattle, wire, and water. They didn't drive herds, they managed empires."

The boy wrote something in his notebook, then asked, "Was that after the Long Drives?"

"It was," the old man said. "After the trails died and the rails took over. The last big herd went up the Chisholm Trail in the late '80s. After that, the cattle stopped movin' and the world started comin' to them. The barbed wire made the change, and the **railroads** finished it. A man could load beef on a train in Abilene or Fort Worth and have it on a dinner plate in Chicago before the dust settled back home. That changed everything."

He took a slow pull on his pipe. "The cowhands still rode, but they weren't ridin' for freedom anymore. They worked for outfits so big a man could ride all week and still be on the same ranch. **King Ranch**, **XIT**, **Waggoner**, **Four Sixes**, those weren't spreads, boy, they were nations with their own laws. The brands were more powerful than county lines."

He smiled faintly. "Each ranch had its mark. The **Running W** of King Ranch, the **Four Sixes**, the **Double D** of the Waggoner. Those brands were burned deep into the hides and the hearts of every man who worked 'em. You could tell a ranch's story just by lookin' at its brand. Some were made from letters, some from numbers, but all were carved from pride."

The old man tapped the pipe against his boot heel. "The open range was gone, and not everyone took kindly to it. The old-timers missed the wild country. They said wire was the death of the cowboy. Maybe it was. But it was also the birth of somethin' new, a Texas that could stand on its own feet and feed the world."

He leaned back in the chair. "The barons didn't just buy cattle; they bought land, lots of it. When a man could get title to land, he could borrow against it. Banks trusted land, and land turned cattle into business. That's when ranchin' stopped bein' a way of life and turned into an empire."

He looked off toward the dark, where the prairie stretched out past the edge of sight. "They were a hard breed, those cattle kings. Some started poor, some had a little help, but they all gambled against drought and wind. A bad year could wipe out a fortune faster than a good year could build it. And when a man lost his herd, he had to look his hands in the eye and tell 'em they'd been ridin' for nothin'. That's a kind of shame you don't get over."

The boy asked, "Did they get along?"

The old man laughed softly. "As much as kings ever do. They fought over water rights, grazing land, markets, and pride. But they all needed the same thing, the **railroads**. Those rails were the veins of the new Texas, carryin' beef north and lifeblood back south. Every town that lived had a depot. The ones that didn't, died quiet. You can still find the bones of some of 'em out there, old storefronts and wells, the ghosts of towns that missed the tracks by a mile."

He took the pipe from his mouth. "So when you hear that train whistle at night, remember, that's the sound that ended the old Texas and started the new one. The wind still blows, the grass waves, but the land belongs to men who traded saddles for ledgers."

The boy wrote one last note, then asked, "What were their names?"

The old man's eyes narrowed with memory. "**Richard King**, down on the coast. **Mifflin Kenedy** beside him. Up north, the **XIT Company**, big enough to buy a Capitol. Out west, **W.T. Waggoner** and **Burk Burnett** who built the **Four Sixes**. They were the last men who thought big enough for Texas."

He smiled faintly, pipe smoke driftin' upward. "They fenced the land, but they couldn't fence the sky. That part still belongs to the wind."

Richard King and the Kingdom of the South

The old man drew slowly on his pipe. "Way down south," he said, "where the brush country meets the river, there's land that looks half wild even now. That's where a man named **Richard King** built himself a kingdom. He did it earlier than the others, before the Civil War."

He tapped ash over the porch rail. "King wasn't born to it. Came here by water, workin' steamboats on the **Rio Grande** with another fella named **Mifflin Kenedy**. Both of 'em Yankees, both sharp with numbers, both seein' a chance in this rough country. They hauled freight, soldiers, cotton, whatever would float. When the war with Mexico ended, King rode inland lookin' for somethin' more solid than a boat. Found grass, found water, and figured that was all a man really needed."

He paused, lookin' toward the dark. "He bought land along the **Santa Gertrudis Creek**. Didn't look like much then, just mesquite and sky, but he could see what others couldn't. Started small, added a little more each year, till that patch of scrub turned into the **King Ranch**."

The old man smiled faintly. "King was tough but smart enough to know he couldn't do it alone. Brought in whole families from across the river. Called 'em the **Kineños**, his men, his people. They stayed, worked, raised kids right there. When they died, the next ones took their saddles. Folks say King built the ranch, but the truth is, they built it for him."

He leaned back. "The ranch near died a few times. He nodded south. "That country'll turn on a man quick," he said. "Drought hit so hard the creeks just up and disappeared. Nothing but dust where the water ought to be. Cattle dropped where they stood, too worn out to look for shade. Now and then raiders came up from Mexico, slippin' in at night, takin' horses and leavin' heartache behind. King saw plenty of it. "When the land started dyin' under him, he changed what he was doin'," the old man said.

"Started diggin' wells where others just packed up and left. Put windmills on the ridges, anything that might keep the grass hangin' on. Broke the range into pieces so it could rest a spell. Folks laughed at him for it, said you can't fence the wild, said the wind don't care about posts and wire. But King just nodded and kept workin'. He figured a man either learned from the land or got buried in it."He just kept at it, hammerin' posts till the calluses split. In the end, he proved 'em wrong and turned out he was right about buildin: something special."

He thumbed the edge of the pipe. "It got to where the place was more like a town than a ranch, school, store, church, its own law. When the war between North and South came, King sided with the South. Lost near everything when it ended. Sold beef to Union camps just to keep the doors open. But he held on, and when the **railroads** reached down from San Antonio, that's what saved him. He loaded beef on trains instead of trails. The iron horse replaced the longhorn drives, and the ranch lived."

The boy asked, "How big was it, Grandpa?"

The old man chuckled. "Big enough that a man could ride three days and still be on it. Over a million acres, give or take, and a brand, **the Running W**, that still means somethin'. The brand resembles a Texas Diamond Back rattler. You see that mark, you're lookin' at a story that never quite ends."

He rubbed his hands together. "When King died, his wife **Henrietta** kept it goin'. Tough lady. Folks tried to buy her out; she told 'em the name wasn't for sale. She ran that ranch tighter than any man ever did. The Kineños stayed with her, loyal as kin."

He looked out toward the yard, pipe smoke driftin'. "The King Ranch was Texas before Texas knew what it wanted to be, stubborn, proud, too big for common sense. They ran cattle, bred horses, and even hit oil later on. Didn't matter what the world changed into, they just kept ridin'. Still do."

The boy scribbled in his notebook. "Was it the biggest?"

The old man shrugged. "Maybe not by numbers, but by spirit, yeah. It was the first one to last. King proved a ranch could be more than luck and weather; it could be a legacy. The men who came after him—**Waggoner**, **Burnett**, the **XIT**—they all followed the trail he cut."

He stood, stretched his back, and nodded toward the dark. "Next story's about that XIT, the ranch that traded grass for granite. Bigger than most countries and just as hard to run. We'll take that one tomorrow."

The XIT and the Ten Counties of Dust

The old man rubbed the edge of his pipe against the porch rail, slow and careful. "If King Ranch was the heart of Texas cattle," he said, "then the **XIT** was the bones. It held up the whole Panhandle."

He leaned back. "Most folks don't know it started with a swap. The **State of Texas** needed a new Capitol building. They wanted granite, ironwork, and skilled labor, and none of that came cheap. So the state offered somethin' else instead, land. Three million acres of it. Ten counties in the Panhandle, near all of it wild and wind scoured. A Chicago company took the deal, built the Capitol in **Austin**, and got itself the biggest cattle spread the world had ever seen."

He let out a low whistle. "They called it the **XIT Ranch**, that meant 'Ten in Texas,' though some folks said it stood for 'Extra in Trouble.' Either way, it fit. The ranch stretched near two hundred miles north to south, longer than some countries are wide. A man could start ridin' at dawn and not see the far fence for many nights."

He looked off toward the plains. "They ran **150,000 head** in the good years. Had cow camps every twenty or thirty miles, a blacksmith, cook, and remuda at each one. The riders lived rough, same as the trail days, just fenced in now. Their pay was low, their work never ended, and the wind was their only company. They said the sun never set on the XIT, but that was just another way of sayin' the work never stopped."

He took a pull from his coffee. "Up north, that land was flat as an old table and just as empty. The grass grew high, but the storms rolled higher. A man could watch a thunderhead form in the morning and still be ridin' under it by night. Lightning killed cattle and cowboys both. Fires raced across those plains fast enough to burn a man out of his saddle."

The boy looked up. "Did it make money?"

The old man snickered, dry and low. "For a time, those city folks just thought they knew it all," he said. "Sittin' up north behind desks, pushin' papers, think they could run a ranch with telegrams and spreadsheets. Sure, they knew numbers, but not the terrain. Could not feel which way the wind was shifting or catch sight (or scent) of rain in the air. Out here, the earth doesn't acknowledge neckties. One year, the clouds stopped coming." Sky went white. That's when they learned what Texas does to men who think they can outsmart her."When it was over, they started sellin' what was left, little at a time, till there wasn't much more to sell." Still, it left its mark. Every town from **Dalhart** down to **Hereford** grew up under that brand's shadow."

He knocked his pipe clean. "That's the other thing folks forget, the **railroads** built the XIT as much as the cattle did. "The **Fort Worth and Denver City** line cut straight through that country," he said. "The **Santa Fe** came in from the other side. Every siding turned into a camp, and the camps grew into towns. Before long, those towns were markets. A man could load a herd at one spur and see the beef sold in **Kansas City** before the week was done. That's what the rails did, they made ranchers into merchants.

Without 'em, the herds would've just stood out there and starved on their own shadows."

He scratched the stubble on his chin. "It wasn't just cattle that moved on those rails. They carried fence posts, flour, and mail, lifelines for the men who rode the range. Before the rails, the Panhandle was a lonely, deadly place. After, it was just lonely."

He laughed softly. "You know, some say the XIT was cursed. Too big to run, too far to guard. There were rustlers, always. Every herd big enough to see from the next hill had somebody tryin' to trim it down. They hired Rangers, Pinkertons, and more riders than some armies, but you can't fence off greed. The wind carries it the same as dust."

He looked at the boy. "But you gotta hand it to 'em, they tried. They built windmills where the hand dug wells ran dry, strung telegraph wire across the emptiest country God ever made. When a blizzard hit, they lit lanterns on the fences so riders could find their way back to camp. And they kept ridin', no matter how bad it got. Men like that don't make headlines, but they make history."

The boy was quiet for a long time. Then he asked, "What happened to it?"

"Time," the old man said. "Same thing that happens to everything big and proud. The XIT went broke in the early nineteen-hundreds. The land was sold off in chunks, the fences rusted, and the brand faded into memory. But the country it covered, that stayed. Still ranches up there, still cattle, still wind strong enough to lean on. The XIT just taught 'em how to work it."

He pointed with his pipe. "Out of that land came towns. **Channing**, **Bovina**, **Texline**, **Dalhart**, all grew where the rails stopped long enough to fill a water tank. Those rails were the lifeblood, boy."The trails were done for," he said. "The trains took over and kept Texas breathin'. Without those rails, the Panhandle would've just blown clear off the map."

He eased back in his chair. "That's the XIT, ten counties of fence, dust, and sky. Too big to last, but it showed folks what Texas could look like if a man dared to dream that high. Even broke, it left pieces behind—some towns, a few stories, and a reminder that nobody ever truly owns the wind."

He looked toward the horizon, where the first stars were showin'. "Next came the new barons, **Waggoner**, **Burnett**, men who turned oil and cattle into one fortune. They weren't just dreamin' in acres; they were thinkin' in dynasties."

He gave the boy a nod. "We'll talk about them next. Big spreads, and bigger plans, and the Four Sixes that burned hotter than any brand in the state."

The Four Sixes and the Waggoner: The Plains Empires

The old man knocked the ashes from his pipe and squinted toward the horizon. "By the time the **XIT** was just a story folks told over coffee," he said, "there were still a couple of outfits out west big enough to make a man feel small. The **Four Sixes** was one of 'em. The **Waggoner** was the other. You could ride till your horse went lame and still be inside their fences. Big places, run by men who were thinkin' way down the road, long after they'd be gone."

He rubbed his thumb over the pipe bowl. "That Sixes outfit started with **Burk Burnett**. Some say he won his first herd playin' cards; some say he just worked harder than anybody else. However it started, he made it stick. Built his spread up around Guthrie, hard country, dry and honest. Folks said grass wouldn't grow there, but he proved it would if you gave it a chance. He bred tough cattle and better horses, the kind that could go all day and still have enough left to run at sundown."

The old man leaned forward. "Burnett didn't run the place from some fancy office. He rode the line, same as the rest of 'em. His brand, **6666**, burned deep. When he died, his daughter **Anne** took over. People doubted her at first, like they always do, but she kept that ranch alive through drought and the Depression. Still standin' today, and that brand still means somethin'."

He paused a long while, then went on. "Up north sat the **Waggoner Ranch**. Started by **Dan Waggoner** before the war and grown by his son **W.T.** afterward. Half a million acres, give or take. They ran cattle, raised horses, and when the smell of oil came up through the mesquite, they drilled for that too. They had sense enough to see Texas was changin' and rode the change instead of fightin' it. The **railroads** helped. When the line reached **Wichita Falls**, the Waggoners had their own siding. Beef went out by the carload, oil by the barrel. They even sold a few racehorses just for pride."

"They weren't perfect, not by a long shot," he said. "Those old barons had their faults, like everybody else. But they left things behind that outlived the men themselves. The dirt they turned still grows grass, still feeds stock. The brands they burned into hides a hundred years ago still show up at sales and on gates. Their names faded some, but the work they did stuck." You drive through **King County** or **Wichita County** today, and you'll still see those names stamped on gates and water tanks."

"Another man that made his mark was Sam Maverick, a signer of the Texas Constitution in '36." The old man grinned, " He said he hated branding cattle because it caused the poor cow pain, many think it was so he could claim any unbranded cow as his. To this day, unbranded calves are still called mavericks."

He pointed his pipe toward the west. "They saw what was comin'. Didn't fight it, just tried to stay ahead of it. That's what kept 'em standin' when others folded. They turned drought and dust into legacies."

He gave a quiet laugh. "You won't read much about 'em in the papers now, but every steak off a Texas cow and every saddle horse worth ridin' owes a little somethin' to those folks. They finished what **Richard King** started, made ranchin' more than survival. They turned it into Texas itself."

Fences, Rails, and the End of the Horizon

The lantern burned low, its light wavering in the wind. "That's how it ended," he said. "The open range turned into pastures, and the wild turned into work. The rails stitched Texas together, mile by mile, till even the loneliest stretches had a whistle instead of a coyote callin'."

He let the pipe rest cold beside him. "You'd think with all them fences and rail lines, the trouble would've stopped. It sure didn't.

Down along the **Rio Grande**, cattle still crossed back and forth, and not always with permission. Some called it rustlin', others called it reclaimin'. Either way, it kept both sides busy. The barbed wire might've tamed the plains, but it never tamed the border."

The old man looked toward the south, where the night always seemed darker. "Those raids went on for years. Didn't matter how many Rangers they sent or how many soldiers rode patrol. Herds disappeared in the dark, rifles cracked across the river, and by morning both sides had stories ready. It was half war, half habit. Some say it ran clean into the twenties, maybe later.

He drew a breath. "So while the ranches got bigger and the owners got richer, the old ways never truly quit. A few still settled things with a rope and a Winchester. That's the part folks forget, Texas might've been changin', but it never changed all at once. There was always a stretch of country where time just didn't listen."

He rubbed his thumb over the coffee cup's rim. "The big outfits, King, Waggoner, Burnett, they made ranchin' into business. But down south, across that river, it was still the old game. Cattle moved at night, hooves muffled, dust hangin' in the moonlight. You could call it crime, or you could call it tradition, dependin' on which side of the fence you were standin'."

He looked out at the stars, now sharp against the black sky. "That was Texas in a nutshell, new and old wrestlin' under the same moon. The barons brought money, the rails brought progress, but the border kept its own kind of wild. Some say it still does."

He knocked the pipe empty and set it aside. "Those old ranches stand yet; their names carved into wind and stone. The brands still burn, the cattle still graze, but if you listen close on a quiet night, you can still hear what came before, the sound of hooves crossin' a river that never learned how to stay put."

He poured the last of the coffee into his cup and raised it a little toward the dark. "Tomorrow we'll talk about the rails," he said. "Iron veins, they were. Without the railroads, them barons would've been dreamin' alone. The trains kept Texas breathin', and maybe they still do."

He gave a small nod to the horizon. "To the land," he said, "and to the men still ridin' somewhere out there, followin' the dust."

Chapter Fifteen

Iron Veins, Rails Across Texas

The Whistle in the Dark

The whistle was heard first, a long, low cry that carried across the flats. The old man waited till the echo had faded before he spoke.

"There was a time that sound meant somethin'," he said. "And the first time I heard it, I thought the sky had split open. Turned out it was just Texas learnin' to move faster, railroads had come to the area I lived in."

He thumbed the bowl of his pipe. "Before the rails, the world was slow, wagons and oxen, stage lines if you could pay. Folks lived and died within the distance a horse could ride. Then one day iron wheels started rollin' out of Houston, and nothin' was the same again."

He looked toward the dark, like he could still see the headlight glowin'. "The trains came in the 1850s, short stretches at first, like the Buffalo Bayou, Brazos, and Colorado line. After the war, they kept comin': the MKT, the Santa Fe, the Texas & Pacific, the Southern Pacific. Steel reached places even the Comanche hadn't bothered with. And where the track stopped, towns grew."

He smiled a little. "Most every town that lived in those days had the track runnin' right beside Main Street. Depot first, saloon next, feed store close enough to smell the grain. You could step off the coach and buy a hat, a drink, and a hammer without movin' fifty yards. If the rails missed you by a mile, you were done for. There's still ghost towns out west that died waitin' on a depot."

The boy leaned forward. "Was it really that big a deal?"

"Bigger, remember the early roads were just opportunities for mud pits" the old man said. "It was life itself. Rails meant trade. Cotton went east, cattle north, lumber anywhere it would sell. They brought back tools, cloth, and folks with new ideas. It shrank Texas. Made it feel possible."

He drew on his pipe, the coal burnin' dull red. "You'd see the trains come in at night, lanterns swingin', smoke hangin' over the roofs. Kids would chase alongside till the brakeman shooed 'em off. Whole families waited just to watch the cars unload. Boxes of goods, barrels of flour, maybe a crate of books or a piano if somebody'd been lucky back east. A rail town smelled like coal smoke, grease, and hope."

He chuckled. "The depot was the heart of it all. Every telegram, every ticket, every piece of news came through that little office. When the whistle blew, storekeepers shut their ledgers and headed for the platform. Didn't matter if the train was stoppin' or not, it was company in a lonely place."

The old man shifted, the chair creaking in the quiet. "It wasn't just business. The trains carried people who'd never seen Texas before. Drummers sellin' notions, soldiers, immigrants, runaways. They came off those cars lookin' around like they'd landed on the moon. Some stayed, some left, but all of 'em changed the towns they touched."

He looked at the boy. "That's when time changed, too. Before the rails, a man kept his watch by the sun. After, he kept it by the timetable. Noon was whenever the train said it was. Folks started measurin' their lives between whistles."

The boy asked, "Did everyone like it?"

"Not at first," he said. "Old-timers said the trains scared off the buffalo and brought trouble. Maybe they were right. But they also brought doctors, teachers, and mail. You take the bad with the good, same as always."

He poured coffee from the pot sitting by his boot. "Those rails were Texas' veins, boy. They pumped life into places the wind had almost forgotten. The whistle meant the world still remembered you."

He took a sip, slow and careful. "Funny thing, though, progress never stops where you want it to. The trains made us rich for a spell, but they also made us restless. Once you can go anywhere, stayin' put starts to feel smaller."

He nodded toward the south. "That's how it was. The iron came, and the dust settled around it. Every boardwalk and depot was built from that sound. Even now, when the wind's right, you can still hear it, a long note in the dark, tellin' you Texas is awake."

Rails and Main Street

"Every town hugged the track," the old man said. "Couldn't risk bein' far from it. The depot was always the first thing they built. Then came the stores, the cafe, maybe a hotel if somebody had money. Everything faced the line. Folks wanted to see the train come in."

He spat into the yard. "At sundown, you'd find wagons stacked near the platform. Cotton bales, beef sides hangin' in the shade, women waitin' for letters or kin. That whistle meant life, payday, mail, sometimes bad news, but news all the same."

He scratched at his chin. "Before the rails, people counted distance in days. After, it was hours. The train shrank the map. What used to take a week with a team, you could do before dark if the track held."

The boy asked how a place got started.

"Easy," the old man said. "Wherever the track stopped. A siding turned into a depot, and a depot turned into a town. You missed the line by a mile; you were finished before you started. The railroads selected spots they thought would bring them the best freight business., but that wasn't every little wide spot in the prairie. There are still boards out west from towns that died waitin' on a stop."

He poured coffee slowly. "The section gang kept the rails straight, five, six men swingin' hammers all day. They called them Gandy Dancers, don't know why, sometimes folks hang a name on ya and it just sits there, stuck like. Hard work, sunburned men. They didn't talk much, but they were the reason trains ran on time."

He looked toward the dark street. "Everything in town owed somethin' to that train. The grocer got his flour, the hardware man his nails, even the undertaker his pine boxes. When the freight car rolled in, everybody lent a hand. Kids climbed on the platform just to touch a crate marked *Chicago* or *St. Louis.*"

He gave a dry laugh. "A depot could smell like coal one minute and onion the next, dependin' on what they unloaded. That's how the world reached us, one freight car at a time."

For a bit, he didn't say anything. Then, quietly: "The rails gave us neighbors. You could ride two towns over and still see the same faces. Made the state feel smaller, friendlier maybe. But it cost us somethin'. The cattle trails faded. Telegraph poles cut through the mesquite. Some old hands said Texas was losin' herself. Maybe they were right."

He rubbed the rim of the cup. "Still, when a whistle drifted over the cotton fields at night, it didn't sound like loss. It sounded like a promise. That's what kept folks buildin' along the line."

The Cities That Grew from Steam

The boy asked, "What happened when the rails hit the big towns?"

"Big towns?" the old man said, grinning. "There weren't any till the rails showed up. Remember big places need lots of food, nails, coal oil, and all of the things that a city will use to grow and get bigger, the rails brought those and took away what the area produced to sell."

He tapped the ashes from his pipe. "Take **Fort Worth**. Used to be a sleepy army post and a few traders sittin' by the river. When the rails rolled in from the east, that post turned into a market overnight. They built pens, yards, and chutes right by the line. Cattle that once walked all the way to Kansas got loaded there instead. Before long, the air smelled of beef, smoke, and money."

He chuckled. "The **Stockyards** came later, big as a town by themselves. You could stand on Exchange Avenue and watch trains carry Texas beef clear to Chicago. That's why folks started callin' Fort Worth the place 'where the West begins.' It wasn't poetry. It was business."

He looked toward the boy's notes. "**Dallas** came up different. She was a cotton town before the war, but when the rail junction hit, she sprouted brick buildings faster than mesquite after rain. The **Houston & Texas Central** from the south, the **Texas & Pacific** from the east, both met right there. Banks followed the tracks, and newspapers followed the banks. By 1900, she had telephones, street-cars, and women wearin' hats from New York. Rails made her city minded."

He rubbed the pipe stem between his fingers. "**San Antonio** was older than all of 'em, but even that old Spanish town changed when the Southern Pacific tied her to the coast. The Alamo still stood quiet, but the trains filled the plazas with tourists and soldiers. They came for the missions and left with postcards. Progress always finds a way to sell itself."

The boy smiled. "What about Houston?"

"Houston was born for the rails," the old man said. "She already had the bayou and the port, but the trains made her lungs. Cotton, oil, timber, everything that could roll, rolled through her. By the time the rest of the state was thinkin' about progress, Houston was already runnin' on it."

He poured another half-cup of coffee. "The same story played out everywhere. Little sidings turned into cities, **Abilene**, **San Angelo**, **Temple**, **Tyler**, **Wichita Falls**. The depot was the first courthouse, the first church, and sometimes the only reason to stay. Every whistle meant a chance."

He scratched the back of his neck. "Some towns didn't make it. The track curved a few miles away, and that was enough."You can still spot the bones if you roll slow," he said. "Old footings, gray boards bleached by the sun, weeds where the platform used to be. That's the bill for progress. It always leaves a few ghosts behind."

He tapped the rail with a fingertip. "The trains did more than raise depots. They raised folks' sights. Farmers quit thinkin' in wagon loads and started shippin' by the car. Ranchers learned ledgers, not just ropes. And every now and then, some storekeeper with big ideas ended up runnin' the town."Texas stopped bein' scattered and started actin' like one big piece of land again."

The boy looked up from his writing. "Was everyone happy about it?"

"Not hardly," the old man said. "Some missed the silence. Said the whistle scared the stars away. Maybe it did. But those same folks were the first ones to meet the train when they needed medicine or mail. You can't eat nostalgia, boy. You feed your family with what moves."

He gave a slow nod toward the dark. "The rails made Texas grow up. They tied the coast to the caprock, the pine woods to the plains. The cities still breathe to that rhythm. You stand in downtown Dallas or Fort Worth and close your eyes; you can still hear the hum under the concrete. That's the old heartbeat of the iron veins."

He smiled faintly. "Tomorrow, we'll finish it, the last of the great booms. When the trains met the oil rigs, and the ground itself started talkin'."

CHAPTER SIXTEEN

The Black Gold Rush

The Smell of Riches

The old man poured a little more coffee and looked toward the horizon. "You could smell it before you saw it," he said. "Sharp, heavy, like tar and thunder mixed together. Folks didn't know what to call it at first. Some said it was just bad water. Others said it was the smell of money tryin' to crawl out of the ground."

He chuckled softly. "That smell started a new kind of stampede. Cattle and cotton built the early Texas, but **oil** changed it forever." He settled back, pipe in hand. "It started quiet, way out east near **Nacogdoches**, in the 1860s. Fella drilled for water and hit oil instead. Didn't make headlines, but it lit the fuse. Later came **Corsicana** in the 1890s, the state's first real producing field. They'd been diggin' wells for water there, too, and when the black stuff bubbled up, folks realized the world had shifted under their boots."

He gave a dry laugh. "They said the town smelled like money and brimstone. Within a year, every farmer with a shovel was a wildcatter. Some struck it rich, most just struck rock. But once you see oil come out of the ground, you can't unsee it."

He tapped his pipe against the step. "Then came **Spindletop**, down near **Beaumont**, in 1901. That one changed everything. When that gusher blew, it shot higher than any church steeple in Texas. Covered the sky in mist and oil till the ground ran black. They say it flowed a hundred thousand barrels a day. Changed the map overnight. Ranch land turned into fields of derricks, and the sound of lowin' cattle got replaced by the grind of engines."

The boy frowned. "Didn't that ruin the land?"

"Some of it," the old man said. "They drilled where they shouldn't, spilled more than they saved. But people were hungry for somethin' new. You have to remember, this was a state full of dreamers. When oil came, they didn't see mud and fire, they saw the future."

He smiled faintly. "**Burkburnett, Electra, Ranger, Desdemona**, those were the next big ones. Towns that had been quiet cow stops turned into madhouses overnight. Canvas tents, saloons, and bootleg whiskey as far as you could walk. A man could wake up broke and go to bed rich, or the other way around. Some of those boomtowns lasted; most didn't. But for a few years, it felt like lightning had struck and everyone was tryin' to catch the sparks."

The boy jotted notes quick, lookin' up now and then. "Did any of the old ranchers get into it?"

The old man nodded. "Most of 'em, sooner or later. **W.T. Waggoner**, **Burk Burnett**, even the King Ranch crowd, when oil started showin' up under their pastures, they drilled. Some said they were sellin' out. I figure they were keepin' up with the times. The same men who'd fenced the wind learned to bottle it." He drew a breath. "The oil rush brought a different kind of cowboy. No spurs, no horse, just grease under his nails and fire in his eyes. They called 'em wildcatters. Men who'd risk their last dime and their next breath on the chance of hittin' black gold. Some ended up with whole companies named after 'em. Others vanished in the mud."

He stared into the dark a long time before speaking again. "The booms didn't last forever. Nothin' that loud ever does. But they left behind a new Texas, cities where prairies used to be, refineries where the buffalo once stood. The sky got a little darker, but the lights stayed on."

He smiled at the boy. "Cattle, rails, oil, that's the story in three parts. Each one louder than the last, each one changin' the land a little more. We learned to dig deeper, drive faster, and dream bigger. But in the end, it was still the same Texas, dust, pride, and folks who won't quit."

He lifted the cup in a small salute. "Tomorrow, we'll talk about what came after. The men who thought oil would last forever, and the ones who already knew it wouldn't."

The Boomtowns

The boy looked up from his notes. "What were those boomtowns really like?"

The old man grinned, eyes half shut. "Loud," he said. "Loud and fast and filthy rich, sometimes all in the same hour. When oil hit, towns grew quicker than weeds. You'd see a field one week, and by the next it was tents, shacks, and derricks stretchin' to the horizon."

He tapped his pipe against the step. "First came the wildcatters, then the drillers, then the rest, gamblers, cooks, preachers, and women tryin' to feed families or find fortune. The air buzzed with hammerin' and engines, smelled of grease, sweat, and cheap whiskey. Mud thick as stew. You could lose a boot or a paycheck before noon."

He smiled, eyes far away. "At **Spindletop**, it got so crowded you couldn't walk ten feet without bumpin' into a stranger with a dream. **Beaumont**, **Burkburnett**, **Ranger**, **Desdemona**, **Electra**, every one of 'em had the same fever. A few got rich, most just got tired."

He took a breath and leaned back. "Every boomtown had the same story. Streets laid out crooked, saloons on every corner, and a tent that passed for a bank. Men lined up to buy leases they didn't understand, sellin' tomorrow for a dollar today. When the well hit, you'd hear the shout clear across town. Folks dropped whatever they were doin' and ran to see it gush. Looked like the earth itself was bleedin' joy."

The boy asked, "Did people stay?"

"Some," the old man said. "Most didn't. When the oil slowed, the money ran off just as quick as it came. A boomtown could disappear faster than a snowflake in August. The smart ones packed before the music stopped. The rest stayed and tried to make towns out of the wreckage."

He rubbed the pipe bowl with his thumb. "Not all of it was greed. Some came because they had nothin' left to lose. Farms gone to dust, cattle markets dead. Oil was hope, and hope'll draw a crowd anywhere. Preachers called it providence. Bankers called it progress. The men in the fields just called it a paycheck."

He looked toward the boy. "A roughneck's life wasn't easy. He'd spend twelve hours on the rig, bathed in sweat and oil. Hands cut from the cable, lungs full of smoke. The pay was better than farmin', but the risk was worse. Derricks blew. "Some nights those rigs shook till you swore the earth was comin' apart," he said. "Iron bangin', timbers crackin', men hangin' on and hopin' the cable held. When somebody got hurt, or worse, there wasn't time for speeches. Maybe a hat pulled down, maybe a few words, then back to the noise. That's just how it went. Work didn't stop for sorrow. Roughnecks that could count ten fingers were few."

He rubbed a hand over his face. "But there was pride in it, no denyin'. They weren't just punchin' holes; they were buildin' somethin', even if nobody could name it yet. Sweat, noise, danger, all of it turned into respect somehow. A few of those roughnecks made it clear to the top, drillers, pushers, even owners, before it was done." Texas always did have a way of turnin' workin' men into legends."

He chuckled. "There were good times, too. Saturday nights in those boom camps were a sight, fiddles playin', money changin' hands faster than cards, laughter spillin' out of every tent. Folks forget that part when they talk about the oil days. They think it was all greed, but there was fellowship in the middle of it. Everyone was hungry for the same thing, a better tomorrow."

He looked out into the dark. "A few of those towns lived on. Some small like Burkburnett, Electra, and Corsicana, and others larger, **Beaumont**, **Kilgore**, **Midland**, **Odessa**, they made the jump from boom to business. Built banks, schools, and courthouses. Others went quiet, left to the tumbleweeds. But if you stand in the right place when the wind shifts, you can still smell the oil in the dirt. It never leaves."

He took a sip of cold coffee. "That was the boom. Fast, noisy, wild, and gone before you knew it. But it changed everything. Turned Texas from cattle and cotton to engines and ambition. The dust got darker, but the future got brighter."

He emptied the dregs of his coffee into the yard. "Every boom burns out," he said. "Oil was no different. Once the quick wells were done, the big outfits took over. Wildcatters sold what they'd found to men with money in banks up north. The camps went quiet, the tents came down, and offices went up. The oil patch started wearin' a collar."

He rolled the pipe between his hands. "That's when the barons showed up. Names folks still toss around, **Hunt**, **Hughes**, **Cullen**, **Kemp, Kell**, and plenty more. They built refineries where grass used to be. You could see the glow of the fires for miles, smell the gas even farther. Towns like **Beaumont**, **Houston**, and **Kilgore** stopped bein' towns. They turned into cities made out of noise and light."

The boy asked if it was good for Texas.

"Hard to say," the old man answered. "It brought jobs, sure. Money too. But moneys like oil, it runs wherever it wants. Neighbors fought over land. Families split over leases. Some struck it rich. Others lost the dirt under their boots."

He shifted, the chair creakin'. "It changed things, though. The rails had stitched the state together, but oil filled it. Paid for roads and schools, even hospitals. Made cities breathe faster. You can thank the wells for the lights that never go out."

He paused to light his pipe again. "By the twenties, you had men rich enough to buy counties. Some spent it all on cars and big houses. Others just stayed quiet and let the checks pile up. Folks called 'em barons, but they weren't so different from the cattle kings. Same hunger, just a new herd to chase."

The boy frowned. "Didn't it hurt the land?"

"It did," the old man said. "Creeks went bad, grass died, air got heavy. But this country's tough. Give it time and a little rain, it'll come back around."

He looked out across the dark. "After a while, the whole state ran on oil. Cattle still grazed, trains still whistled, but the pumps kept the lights on. The barons said it was progress. Maybe it was. Maybe it was just the same story again, men takin' what the land offered and callin' it success."

He drew a long breath. "You can still see what they built. Refineries down by the coast, pump jacks nodding in the sun, and cities that don't know what quiet sounds like. That's their monument."

He turned to the boy, a tired smile on his face. "Someday the wells'll dry, same as the herds and the trails before 'em. But the land'll still be here. Always is. She just waits for the next fool who thinks he can own her." He looked towards the horizon, "Boy, the horse and mule have served man for nigh onto thousands of years, someday, this fad will fade when man decides to slow down and smell the wind."

Epilogue

The Last Lesson

The porch is quiet now. The old chair still sits in the same spot, worn smooth where a man's hands once rested. The air carries that familiar smell of mesquite smoke and far-off rain.

The old man is gone, claimed by time, same as the cattle, the rail, and the oil booms he used to talk about. But the boy remains, grown gray around the edges himself. He stands by the rail and stares at a faded photograph in his hand. It's the two of them, side by side, coffee cups between them, the world behind them wide and bright.

He can still hear the voice. The slow way the old man told things, never hurrying, letting the words roll out like dust on a quiet road. He'd spoken of kings and cowhands, soldiers and dreamers, the proud and the forgotten. Every story carried the same heart, and all of them built Texas.

A shift of wind stirs the dust on the porch. The man looks down and sees it wedged between the boards, an old pipe, the stem cracked, the end chewed near smooth. He kneels, picks it up gently. The smell of ash is long gone, but the memory isn't. A tear wets his cheek before he can stop it.

He sits on the same step the old man used to favor and lets the memories come.

He thinks about how the land had always made its own kind of people. The first dreamers who followed **Austin**, **Houston**, **Crockett**, and the others who turned wilderness into promise. But he also remembers what the old man taught him on this very porch, that Texas was more than those few names written big in books. It was **Seguin**, **Navarro**, and **Menchaca**. It was **Flores**, **Enriquez**, and **Esparza** who stood at the Alamo, just as Travis and Bowie. It was the hands that built fences and rail beds, the women who kept families alive through drought and war, the Black and Mexican laborers who worked fields they didn't own but helped make bloom.

He looks across the yard to the stretch of land turning gold under the last light. "It was never just the generals and the governors," he whispers. "It was everybody."

The wind picks up a little, whispering through the mesquite. Somewhere far off, a train whistle carries on the air, soft, almost like a memory.

The man sets the old pipe back where he found it and gives the chair a slow push with his hand. It creaks once, like it remembers too.

"Thank you," he says to the empty porch. "You were right."

He turns toward the fading sun. The light lies long across the land, open, scarred, stubborn, and beautiful. Texas, still holdin' on, just like the people who built it.

And for a moment, standing there in the quiet, he can almost hear the old man again, drawling out the same truth he'd told a hundred times:

"Son, this place wasn't made by heroes alone. It was made by everyone who ever called it home."

The sound lingers, softer than wind through the mesquite, and the man smiles through his tears. Texas endures, just like the people who remember her.

Acknowledgements

I personally need to thank the makers of Grammarly. That poor program was taxed to the limits with my English skills, and the porch talk of the old man. A drop down would constantly remind me that I should say older adult, as the term old man might be offensive. As an old man, I can say truthfully that it is not offensive to this old man, just reality.

And now to the thanks. Mrs. Bell, her reminders to teach the children well and tell like it was and not how we wish it was. Eric Enriquez and his love of history and all things Texas, Donald and Connie Patty, descendants of great Texas families and most of all to my daughter JoAnn Miller, whose name is with mine on the cover and her tireless treks with her dad to Fort Parker, Richardson, etc. My grandson, James, who often heard the old man talk about history as we explored Fort Laramie, Larned, Robinson etc.

About the author

JW Jones was born in 1948 in Dodge City, Kansas. His given name was Pugh, but that changed after his mother married a Texan named M.H. Jones. In 1960, the family left the vast Kansas prairies and headed south to Texas.

He grew up in **Burkburnett**, a town still carrying the echoes of the old oil boom. Walking those fields as a boy, he could see the black tar patches that clung to the sandy soil and the weathered timbers from long-fallen derricks. Down at *Joe & Joe's Barbershop*, he'd listen to the old-timers swap stories about the boom days, mules lost in the muddy streets, fortunes made and gone before payday. Every man swore he'd seen it happen or knew the one who had. That's Texas for you: where truth and tall tales shake hands so often you can't tell them apart.

In 1965, after years of hearing those porch stories about courage and adventure, Jones joined the **U.S. Navy**, hoping to follow the example of the men who'd come before him. He served four tours in **Vietnam**, three as a door gunner on rescue helicopters, then spent several years traveling the world, living in **Germany** and the **Philippines** before returning home.

Using the **G.I. Bill**, he earned a degree in **History** from **Midwestern University** in Wichita Falls, Texas. Diploma in hand, he began a long career teaching and coaching in small-town schools, first in **Italy, Texas** (the one with football, not wine), then in **Red Oak** and **Abbott**.

He retired early, at seventy-four, but the stories never stopped. The porch talks of his youth and the history he taught for decades came together in *TALES OF OLD TEXAS,* a blend of memory, legend, and the stubborn pride of a state that still believes its stories matter.

His first work, *MAYDAY, A SAGA of the BIG MOTHERS,* published in 2023, highlighted his squadron mates in the USN helicopter squadron, HS 6, performing rescues in North Vietnam. Since that time, he has worked on a number of projects, many near completion, After *TALES OF OLD TEXAS, WINGS OF VALOR, THE SEADEVILS IN VIETNAM* and *ABOVE AND BEYOND, WHEN I HAVE YOUR WOUNDED* are also near publication.

Private publishing is dependent on Amazon reviews...kindly leave an honest review of this *Tale of Old Texas,* the old man on the porch wouldn't want it any other way.